DAVID METZENTHEN

GEORGE PARKER GOES GLOBAL

ALLEN & UNWIN

SYDNEY · MELBOURNE · AUCKLAND · LONDON

First published by Allen & Unwin in 2018

Allen & Unwin
83 Alexander Street
Crows Nest NSW 2065
Australia
Phone: (61 2) 8425 0100
Email: info@allenandunwin.com
Web: www.allenandunwin.com

A catalogue record for this
book is available from the
National Library of Australia

ISBN 978 1 76052 346 6

For teaching resources, explore
www.allenandunwin.com/resources/for-teachers

Cover design, illustrations & text design by
Astred Hicks, Design Cherry
Set in 12.5/18 pt Bembo by Midlands Typesetters, Australia
Printed in Australia in April 2018 by McPherson's Printing Group

10 9 8 7 6 5 4 3 2 1

The paper in this book is FSC® certified.
FSC® promotes environmentally responsible,
socially beneficial and economically viable
management of the world's forests.

For Kath Pelletti

CHAPTER ONE

Well, it all began with the worst haircut in the world and one unbelievable (especially to me) three-point shot. Where it will end, I don't know – but what I do know, *now*, is that if someone asks you to dance, you dance. Especially at Madison Square Garden in New York City in the United States of America. You'll see what I mean.

My mother once said I was blessed with brains but got a little bit lost on the way to the good looks department. Staring in the mirror of Klassicke Kutz Hair Salon, I can't help but agree. I have a face that reminds me of an uncooked gingerbread man. It's round and pale and my features are like an assortment of dried fruits. Needless to say, I did not get my scholarship to Tapley Grammar Boarding School for being handsome or talented at sport.

My hairdresser, whose name is Maddylynne, holds

up a handful of hair that has grown rather long over the last term. It suits me as I am a logical, scientific, chess-playing, calculator-carrying mathematical type who actually owns a telescope – which I keep carefully hidden under my bed, as the only stars that Tapley Grammar boys generally look at are action-movie heroes who have lots of guns, cars and girlfriends, but not many clothes.

'This has gotta go, Georgie-boy.' Without warning, Maddylynne swoops with the clippers, leaving what looks like a narrow dirt road through a crop of wheat on the right side of my head. 'Your school likes it *short*.' Then she turns the narrow dirt road into a superhighway. 'There. That's what I'm talking about! This haircut is going to last all summer long.'

She's not wrong. Half my head looks like a roast potato. The other half looks like the edge of a frayed doormat. And it is at this point that the fire begins behind the curtain leading to the mysterious back room where all the ladies go to get their legs – and other things – waxed.

'Geez, I'm sorry, George.' Maddylynne unplugs the clippers and puts them in her apron pocket. 'But we'd better abandon ship.'

So, with five waxy, partly undressed ladies, I go outside and watch the Klassicke Kutz Hair Salon burn to the ground. Then I walk back to school, knowing that my life at Tapley Grammar is about to get a hundred times tougher because I see the ultra-wealthy and super-talented Chase Landon-Bond playing one-on-two basketball and probably winning. And Chase has seen me.

To be more precise, he has seen my haircut.

Both sides of it.

The basketball game stops. But I continue onwards, a dead man walking on a perfectly raked gravel path taking me to the end of my life as surely as a pirate's plank.

'Well, well, *well*,' says Chase Landon-Bond, whose family are *extremely* rich. 'I don't know what has inspired this rather . . .' He spins the ball on a fingertip, 'space-age hair-*do*, George Parker, but that's the most unbelievably cool hair*style* I have ever seen. I am *impressed*.' Then he smiles, with blindingly white teeth.

Now, as surely as the square root of one hundred and sixty-nine is thirteen, I know George Parker is *not* cool. Rather, I'm the quite-bright-but-not-quite-right (according to my Tapley Grammar counsellor) only child of scientist parents who are in a Swiss bunker with a box of moon rocks, theorising about a collision between planet Theia and Earth – and as this collision happened four *billion* years ago, I wouldn't think they'll be reaching any conclusions any time soon, which means I'll be spending the summer holidays at school, suffering at the hands of the more wealthy students like a mouse in a lab that develops rat poison.

'Er, thanks, Chase,' I say, waiting for the trap to spring and steel jaws to crush my neck.

With a flick of his golden wrist, Chase consults his Limited Edition Tag Heuer sports watch. Then he pushes the basketball hard into my chest.

'Five seconds on the clock, Parker! We're two points down in the NBA playoffs! It's a three-pointer *or* the toilet!'

I don't really play sport. I'm a first-aid volunteer and a ball monitor who can turn his hand to cone-stacking and be relied upon to successfully close storage cupboards, even if they are full of ill-matched sporting equipment, including polo mallets and jousting lances.

'Shoot, George! *Shoot!*' Chase's grey eyes sparkle.

His blond hair is like a wavy halo. 'Put it *up*! Give it *air*! Do your *thang*, George!'

I have no choice. Rich boys at Tapley Grammar (and that is most of them) think they can order the poorer boys around, and they're right, because it's a school rule. So, from the edge of the court, in sheer desperation, I throw the ball at the orange ring that I can hardly see without my glasses. And up the ball goes, down it comes – straight, *unbelievably*, through the net.

For a moment, there's stunned silence. Then Chase Landon-Bond explodes.

'Parker scores!' He drags me, stumbling, up the court. 'It's a buzzer-beater! It's extraordinary! Yes, the normally *hopeless* George Parker *wins* the game!' Chase twists my chin as if changing a lightbulb. 'Talk to the camera, George! You can't sneak back into your dark soggy box like a sub-normal snail. You've gotta speak to your fans!'

I remember something I saw on TV in the waiting room for Mrs Plunk, my orthotic shoe specialist and one-time role model (until she went to jail for car-jacking).

'Hank,' I say. 'Without them other guys, I'd still be back in Pocatello, Idaho, jest raisin' pumpkins for mah hogs. And I'd like to say how-do to my beautiful wife, Lulu-Rose, and a give a super-loud call-out to mah 'coon dawg, Pancho. Boo yah. Boo yah. We're, er, bringing it home. Bang. Boom, I mean.'

Chase laughs in my face, at the same time shaking me so hard that my teeth click like castanets.

'*Idaho*, George? Your 'coon dog, *Pancho*? Man, you are the funniest kid in *Australia*! And I always thought you were – how can I put this? An idiot.' He slaps me so hard on the back that my asthma inhaler flies out of my pocket. 'Georgie-boy,' he adds, 'this is going to be the summer of your life. Or winter, if we end up in the northern hemisphere. Which is possible, as I have a private jet.'

Chase *does* have a private jet. Once, it flew so low over our school that it cracked a stained-glass window in the Tapley chapel that showed Jesus giving a beggar his old iPhone 5.

'*You* sit with *me* at tea tonight, George,' Chase announces. 'We have plans to make. *Big* plans.' He steps back, studying my hair. 'Man, that *style*. *Edgy*? It's off the damn *scale*! You have blown me out of the water.'

That makes two of us.

'Oh,' I stammer. 'You know, sometimes I just do *crazy* things.' I don't. I never do. I never have. It is against all Parker family principles.

Chase nods. His friends, Royal Highness Prince Jimahl, and Count Luciano, simply look mystified. Neither has ever spoken to me, although once Prince Jimahl poked me out of the way with his jewelled umbrella.

'George,' Chase says seriously. 'It's time to stop watching the world from an upstairs window. You've got to be a *player* not a *prune*. You *gotta* get *involved*. See you at dinner.'

I walk away in the sunshine to show I'm not a Factor Fifty–type of person, although I most certainly am. Behind me, I hear Chase's clear voice.

'Wow. That Parkster reminds me of that total mad-man painter, Vincent Van Gogh. He's one *wild* dude!'

Vincent Van Gogh was an artist who actually cut half his ear off, not half his hair – but who am I to say what's crazy and what's not?

Maybe doing everything carefully is as crazy as doing everything without thinking?

Maybe planning years ahead is as crazy as not planning at all?

Maybe I *should* put away my telescope and instead *reach* for the stars?

Maybe this *will* be a beautiful summer?

Imagine that.

CHAPTER TWO

My footsteps echo along the Grand Corridor that takes me through the Grand Doors into the Grand Dining Room. On the walls are the names of old Tapley students who have been prime ministers, fighter pilots, successful pirates, Australian cricket captains, or just plain filthy rich. Our school motto is 'Winners Are Grinners', and although I'm not sure it's a *very* good motto, everyone else seems to like it.

Chase is the only student in the dining room. He sits at a front table reserved for the students whose parents donate land, gold bullion, or unmarked cash to the school. And now, I suppose, he'll tell me that this afternoon's friendliness was just one long joke.

Get it over with, George, I tell myself. *Then go back to your antique sim card collection, telescope, well-worn chess set, and set of sixteen colour-coded ethically sourced cotton face washers.* I give a polite cough.

'Er, evening, Chase.'

Chase stands. 'Peorgie boy! Get your multi-dimensional shock-jock rockin'-the-fashion-world hairstyle down here *right* now.'

I set off towards Chase, who shines like a comet – perhaps US 10 Catalina, which I've seen but never up this close.

'Sit,' says Chase. 'Now, George, you'd better have a double serving of trifle tonight, because you'll need all your strength for what I have planned. Whatever little strength you might have.'

'Er, what've you got planned, Chase?' I detect tremors of fear beneath the generous elastic waistband of my wool-cotton blend (80/20) flannel underpants. 'A great plan is a very good idea, that's what my dad says.'

Chase lounges in the old wooden chair as if it was the most comfortable thing ever.

'Well, I don't have *anything* planned *exactly*,' he says. 'As planning *exactly* is a waste of time. Because we both know the universe has something in mind that will test us out to the *max*.'

I'm not sure that the universe has a mind. Then again, I'm not sure that it doesn't.

'We'll need to pick up a few supplies in town for our adventures,' Chase adds.

My parents forgot my spending money. It's remarkable how absent-minded many scientists are, considering how smart they're supposed to be.

'Supplies?' I ask uneasily. 'What for?'

Chase shrugs. 'For *emergencies*, George. I'm sorry I can't be more specific, but if I knew what these emergencies would be, we'd avoid them. Unfortunately, that's not the case. It's a dangerous world out there. Especially for people like you who don't get out much.'

I'd agree with that.

'Oh, *relax*, Parkie.' Chase folds a napkin embroidered with his initials and family portrait. 'If you can handle that haircut, you can handle anything.'

There's a big difference between handling something you can't avoid – like this haircut – and something you thought was a good idea but turned out to be an utter catastrophe. But it also proves that sometimes bad luck turns out to be good luck, as I wouldn't be sitting here with Chase eating cold beans and brown mashed potatoes if Klassicke Kutz hadn't gone up in smoke.

'It's just you and me, George.' Chase looks around the empty dining room. 'The Prince has gone home to India to train some new elephants to help around the house. And Count Luciano is in Germany buying a new castle for his mother.'

'Oh,' I say. 'Those things sound interesting.'

'I guess so.' Chase shrugs. 'But in my experience, elephants are overrated. Their memories aren't as good as people say and they take up a hell of a lot of room. And the toilets in German castles have stone seats and are often smelly *and* haunted. You and I will have *far* more fun.'

I laugh – I can't help it. I've never really had much fun. Even in kindergarten, I was a serious boy. Little George Parker was always alert in the sandpit for a deadly tunnel collapse and to make sure no rubber dinosaurs were subjected to any rough play that might have sped up their passage to extinction and got the toy box monitor (me) into serious trouble.

'That sounds jolly good,' I say.

Chase's smile is super-bright and his eyes shine like the headlights of a Ferrari.

'And if the fun turns out to be a bit risky, treacherous, or dangerous, who cares?'

'Not me, Chase.' I shrug. 'Not me.' I can't believe I said that. I spend an awful lot of time caring about danger because that's what danger is – *dangerous*!

11

'Right,' says Chase. 'We'll meet at the gates at nine tomorrow morning to get our supplies. Now eat that trifle, George. You look a little pale.'

I blame that on my haircut. And the fact that I avoid the sun between seven in the morning and eight at night, unless there's a solar eclipse or I'm under an umbrella under a shade sail.

'Nine o'clock at the gates.' I carefully synchronise my plastic digital watch with Chase's stainless-steel masterpiece of Swiss watchmaking excellence. 'I'll be there.'

'Yes, George,' Chase says. 'You will be.'

CHAPTER
THREE

That night, in my tiny room above the dark Tapley school grounds, I read an email from my parents. Their moon rock work is going to keep them underground and out of communication for the next month, so they sign off with a smiley face in a test tube, a LOL and a DFTTYSIYU (Don't Forget To Tuck Your Singlet Into Your Underpants). They've also sent me some spending money – in European bank notes, which I can easily exchange for Australian dollars at the Tapley Grammar Four Star Tuckshop and Foreign Currency Exchange.

As I look into the night sky, alone and feeling a little lonely, I see my ever-reliable friends, the stars. In beautiful constellations like Orion, Sirius, and Crux, they map a darkness like the deepest and most mysterious of oceans. In a way, stars remind me of people, all together but separate, each with something to offer – even the dull and distant ones, if anyone bothers to look . . . which has me wondering what I have to offer.

I'd like my talents, if I have any, to be of help to other people. I would like to be someone's good and reliable friend. I would like to be part of the world, rather than orbit around it like Iapetus, the two-toned moon that circles Saturn. In the window's reflection, I see my crazy haircut, leading me to think about the brilliant and brave Chase, and what might happen tomorrow.

Adventures may happen.

Disaster might strike.

Or both, neither, or something in between.

But things *will* happen, because the world is always turning, and we are all turning with it. And that is the indisputable truth.

CHAPTER FOUR

I get to the school gates at nine o'clock. As it's Christmas holidays, Tapley students don't have to wear school uniform. But due to the disturbing fact that my parents think wearing jeans will turn me into a Hell's Angel or a UFC cage fighter, and that my art smock is fine for most social occasions and sporting events, I'm dressed in a George-Parker-Tapley-Grammar outfit of my own creation.

It's made up of antique canvas gym shoes, faded blue floral board shorts that I found in my wardrobe, a white Tapley school shirt, and my Tapley straw hat with its black and gold band. So it's no wonder that the six brass eagles on the school gates seem to look at me strangely, because even the headmaster's German shepherd wears a tailor-made Italian suede jacket with bone-shaped biscuit pockets and a Velcro flap for her Royal German Airlines frequent flyer card.

Chase wanders up the path wearing white jeans, blue sneakers, and a shirt that's a shade of violet

I've never seen before. Sometimes I feel like the super-rich have their own colour spectrums. For instance, you won't see a Tapley boy in seaweed-green, apart from me, unless he's driving a Centurion tank in Cadets, or helping endangered waterbirds to extinction by shooting them out of the sky at the privately owned Lake Tapley Wildlife Reserve.

Chase waves.

'Right on time, Georgie-boy!'

'Ha, yes,' I say. 'No sleeping in today, Chase.' Or any other day, as it's a well-known family story that the last Parker to sleep in was Lawrence Parker in 1932, who earned himself the nickname of Lawrence the Lazy Loser until he died seventy-six years later at work (and in his sleep, funnily enough).

We leave the Tapley school grounds, which include a Formula One practice track, a live ammunition shooting range, and a miniature casino for the preppies. The only sign of life is the Tapley Grammar Commercial Bank, which has the same operating hours as the New York Stock Exchange.

'It's too quiet here over summer,' Chase says. 'Man, time stands still.'

There *is* a feeling of timelessness to the morning,

which is an impossible but rather comical concept to think about if you're a scientific type who's feeling a little down in the dumps.

'Hoo hoo, Chase!' I chuckle out loud. 'That's funny. Time *standing* still.'

Chase gives me a hard look. 'I'm not joking, George. This place is dead. We'll go to my house in the city. It's empty. My parents are away at a Truffle Hunting Boot Camp in France and my sister's in a psychiatric hospital in New York.'

We can't just *leave* school for the holidays!

'Chase,' I say, 'unless our parents sign, counter-sign and sign again a Letter of Agreement, we can't budge. We're stuck.'

'Oh no, we're not,' he replies sternly. 'The head-master will do exactly what my mother tells him. Or he'll find himself as the prime minister again and he won't like that one little bit. Anyway, your parents are down a hole, you said.'

'Yes, they're studying moon rocks in a bunker in Switzerland,' I answer. 'Evidently the rocks are quite heavy.' Which would be no big surprise, I would've thought.

Chase and I walk past the Tapley Grammar Marina and Container-Ship Wharf. Most of the superyachts have gone to the Bahamas for summer, but there are still a couple of the hovercraft that the boys use on the golf course.

'So we won't *disturb* your parents,' says Chase. 'We'll just get on with our own lives.'

That sounds like a very good idea.

'What's that girl doing on the old jetty, George?' Chase looks up the beach, shading his eyes with a golden hand. 'Is she waving at us?'

'She appears to be,' I say. 'D'you know her?'

'Nope.' Chase starts to jog. 'Perhaps she needs help? Come on, George. *Run.*'

We run, which is not something I'm very good at or do very often.

'Pump those arms, George!' Chase whacks my elbow. 'Put some *effort* into it.'

I do, and boy, it does seem to help and I make it onto the jetty a bare thirty metres behind Chase. The girl, who has red hair and is wearing a light-blue dress, points.

'There's a little dog in the water! But I can't swim. Although I'll try, if I have to. Which mightn't turn out so well.'

I can see a little black, white, and brown dog paddling in circles.

'We'll go in.' Chase kicks off his blue sneakers. 'You can swim, can't you, George?'

'Certainly,' I answer. 'I favour the energy-efficient side-stroke that has unfortunately been overlooked as an Olympic event for the last one hundred and forty-eight years.'

'What the——?' Chase shakes his head. 'Just get undressed and get in!'

Despite the fact that I've never undressed in front of a girl before, I remove all non-essential items, as this is an emergency.

'I'll just conduct a quick depth check,' I say, as Chase hops around, trying to get his jeans off. 'It's about ten metres, I estimate, Chase. Not perfect. But I think I can work with an eight-metre margin for error.' And in I go, executing a perfect safety star jump I learned online.

'Go, Georgie!' Chase yells. 'Go!'

I side-stroke steadily. The great advantage of the style is that I can watch the dog and keep my nasal passages clear of water. The threat of shark attack I discount as being mathematically unlikely, but having read a number of disturbing reports of the deadly irukandji jellyfish moving south due to global warming, my pulse rate is in the red zone.

'Swim, George!' The red-headed girl claps. 'You're so brave!'

There's an old Parker-family saying that, 'Bravery is for people with too much time on their hands.' But if what I'm doing is brave, then I'm encouraged, I must say.

The little dog paddles in my direction, crying. Its nose looks like a prune, its eyes like two raisins, so we have that in common.

'Don't worry about the irukandji jellyfish,' I say reassuringly. 'They're still up around the Byron Bay–Maroochydore area. That's two whole states away.' I grab the dog by the scruff of the neck (since it has no collar) and head back to the jetty.

Chase and the girl kneel, ready to help. I give them the little dog and hang on to the jetty, estimating my pulse at about one hundred and ninety.

'Great, George!' Chase peers down. 'That side-stroke is so *weird*, so *stupid*, but you made it. Fantastic!'

I take deep breaths and see that the girl has blue eyes and freckles, and one of her legs is made from plastic that would have a polypropylene core, I'd suggest. 'Your dog, he's—'

'Oh, he's not mine,' she says. 'And he's a she.'

Chase helps me up onto the jetty. 'She's *your* dog now, George. Well done.'

I brush back the hair on one side of my head. Beneath my board shorts, my wool-cotton blend underpants are weighing me down, since they retain as much water as a medium-sized camel.

'I can't have a dog.' I take another breath. 'School rules, Chase. No dogs, cats, or cockatoos. Only polo ponies and leopards, if you have a special permission note from your parents and the African government. And not at my house, either. My mother was traumatised by a miniature schnauzer outside a public library in Munich, and will now allow only a black-and-white poster of a zebra, or a rubber koala on the end of a pencil.'

The girl hands me my Tapley hat, which reminds me that I'm still topless. Good Lord!

'But if you don't take her, George,' the girl shrugs, 'what happens to her?'

I put on my shirt, estimating that I've had enough UV exposure to last until I'm forty-seven years old. With regards to the dog, I have no answer.

'George *can* have her.' Chase stares seawards as if he's to give the order to open fire on a fleet of enemy warships (which many Tapley boys have done, sometimes discovering later that they weren't the enemy after all). 'So that's that. Fixed. She's yours, George. Next!'

By now, the dog has cheered up and is wagging her tail. I daringly put my hand on her shoulder and feel how *alive* she is. Well, maybe I *can* have her!

'You did wonderfully, George.' The red-headed girl smiles. 'Lots of people wouldn't have gone in.'

'Lots of people *would*,' I reply. 'Anyway, I couldn't have done it without you chaps.'

'That's another load of Parker rubbish,' says Chase. 'You showed guts, George. Like a true leader.'

I'm no leader. Most of the time, I can't decide what *I* should do, let alone tell other people. Although as president of the Tapley Chargers Chess Club (known as the T triple C by the coolest of our members), I did move the pencil sharpener away from the door as Stage One of our Risk Management Plan.

The girl stands. I see that the joints in her polypropylene leg are made of titanium, a space-age metallurgical compound. My lunchbox is titanium. My mother says that it will *last a lifetime*, and my dad says, *There's not an aeronautical engineer in this country, George, who would take her to court over that one.*

'My name's Charlotte.' The girl sweeps her hair back in a rippling copper wave. 'What are you going to name your dog, George?'

'Charlotte,' I begin, 'I don't think—'

'Shut up, George.' Chase walks around with his shoelaces undone, which is banned under Stage Two of the Tapley Chargers Risk Management Plan. 'Give the dog a name. I thought you were bright.'

'I'm not bright,' I protest. 'I just happen to be good at maths, chemistry, physics, biology and languages, and have a deep interest in astronomy and fast-acting glues. I'm not good with names. I inherited that from my parents, Olruss and Tedward. I myself am named after a failed IBM computer, the George 1972.'

'How about calling her *Sponge*?' Chase suggests. 'Or Spot? Spotless? Collarless? *Aimless?*'

'*Amy.*' This is the first name that pops into my head. I did consider a few numbers I'm rather fond of, but they'd be difficult to call out in an off-lead park, I would think. 'There. A short name for a short dog.'

Charlotte laughs. 'Oh, George. You're so funny. I'm going to put you in the book I'm writing.'

Book? 'Well, I'm not sure it'll be a particularly funny book,' I say, 'if I'm in it. Because my comic talents are limited to a witty fact-based riddle or a historically accurate limerick shared with the lads at the Tapley Chargers Chess Club. No way am I—'

Chase snaps his fingers. 'Stop saying that you're *not* things when you *are* things, George. Now get Amy, and let's get going. We've got to get organised today to be off tomorrow.'

We say goodbye to Charlotte and leave the jetty, then Chase and I head into town in the bright sunshine, which does nothing to diminish my dark fears for the future. And when I'm fearful, I tend to sneeze, which is what led me to the creation of my Early Warning Hay Fever app called the *Parker Sneezer Wheezer Appeaser*. But my invention was wiped off the online world by the powerful and violent South American crime gang, the Unpleasant Piranhas, who run the multi-billion-dollar illegal tissue trade out of the slums of Panama City.

CHAPTER FIVE

In Lonsdale, Chase and I see a pet shop full of pet things. We enter, taking Amy with us.

'Just get the essentials.' Chase looks around. The place is cluttered with bird cages, dog kennels, tortoise shelters, and bubbling fish tanks. 'Don't go overboard, George.'

I don't know what the essentials are for a dog, but I guess food would be one. And I can't go overboard, as I don't have the 'going overboard' kind of money.

'I'll have some dog food, please,' I say to the lady, who is cross-eyed, so it's hard to say if she's looking at me, Amy or outside. 'For this dog.' I hold Amy up, to make sure the lady is on target.

'Buy it at the supermarket,' she says. 'It's cheaper.'

'Of course,' I agree, as she seems quite definite about it. 'Well, perhaps I'll just have a dog lead and a collar, please.' They would surely be essential equipment for responsible dog ownership.

'Supermarket,' the lady says. 'Cheaper.'

I look at Chase, who shrugs. 'She'll need a top-quality coat, George,' he says. 'Something wind-, water- and snow-proof.'

A coat? That is snow-proof? I look outside. The street is baking under a hot Australian summer sun.

'It's thirty-five degrees, Chase,' I observe. 'Give or take a degree.'

'Not in New York, it's not.' Chase is engrossed by a Mexican walking fish that is swimming in rapid circles. 'Or in Paris.'

I guess I hadn't considered being in either of those two places any time soon.

'We need a dog coat, er, please,' I say to the lady.

'Supermarket,' she repeats. 'Possibly.'

This strikes me as weird, but I suppose a business operator can run her business any way she likes.

'Yes, absolutely,' I say doubtfully. 'Thank you for your help.'

We buy everything we need for Amy from the supermarket and a sale-item sheepskin jacket from a farm supplies store.

'Right,' says Chase. 'Do *you* have a good jacket, George?'

I wear my school blazer in cooler conditions, which is what my mother said it was for. If it's *very* cold, I wear a thermal singlet underneath my school shirt. And if it's *exceptionally* cold, I wear a turtleneck jumper under the blazer but over my shirt. Plus gloves, scarf, and a pom-pom hat, all home-knitted with Australian merino wool.

'I do like the Tapley blazer, Chase.' I see he winces at this. 'Students have been wearing it for over one hundred years with no complaints. Many older folk call it a *rather smart jacket*. Sometimes I'll add a colourful turtleneck jumper with contrasting woollen ear muffs for extra warmth. It's an extremely flexible item, the blazer.'

Chase crosses his arms. 'It wouldn't be too flexible if it was frozen stiff,' he says. 'And neither would you be.'

It would be hard to argue that point, I suppose.

'But I only have thirty-nine dollars left, Chase.'

'Don't worry about money, George,' says Chase. 'I've asked you to come to my house, so you're my guest. And with your brain, we should be able to swing a few deals to cover costs. Anyway, I'll lend you a coat. I have seventy or so. But if you ever wear a turtleneck jumper under it, I will have you killed.'

As some Tapley families do have private armies, threatening to have someone killed is taken quite seriously at school, and might result in a half-hour detention.

'I'm joking,' Chase adds. 'By the way, what colours are your turtleneck jumpers?'

'One is a rather restful shade of dark green,' I say. 'And the other is a very pleasing woodland brown.'

Chase doesn't look too thrilled. At all.

'Not turtle-green, George? Not frog-brown?'

I suppose you could classify the colours as such.

'Kind of a mossy-green,' I suggest hopefully. 'On a brighter day. And perhaps a cheerful chestnut brown. On a sunny morning.'

Chase takes one of my shopping bags. 'George, those colours would be fine if you lived in a pond or under a barn. But if you dress like a piece of damp wood, girls will think you're clammy.'

I agree that looking clammy or like a piece of damp wood would not be ideal.

'Anyway,' Chase continues, 'let's get a coffee. I've got to make a call.' He walks towards an old waterfront building and Amy and I follow.

'Would it be all right if I had tea instead, Chase?' I ask. 'Tea is rather more healthful for the teenaged organs.'

'Tea is rather more *hopeless*,' Chase answers. 'You'll have to get used to coffee if we end up in the United States or Europe.'

The idea of going to America and Europe is alarming. I do have a passport, since visiting the New Zealand Antarctic Centre as winner of the Southern Hemisphere Interesting Teenagers competition – which didn't look very good as an acronym on the trophy. Anyway, the Antarctic Centre was closed, although I did look through a window and saw a scientist making a toasted cheese sandwich while being kept company by a very attentive king penguin.

'Chase, you can't just jump on a plane and turn up in another country.'

'You wanna bet?' Chase pulls out his mobile phone. 'If Clementine is out of bed, we're all set to go.'

Well, that's clarified things – *not* (as some people say – a modern but extremely clumsy way of expressing a negative sentiment). When I said it to my mother during a dispute over asparagus, she was so grammatically confused that she had to lie down.

'Who's Clementine?' I ask as we climb a rickety old staircase.

'Our family pilot,' Chase says. 'She was flying F-18s

for the air force, but missed a few missions because she slept in. Eventually they had to let her go.'

Perhaps I *do* need a cup of coffee?

CHAPTER SIX

Chase and I go into a tiny coffee shop that looks to have been opened in the same year that tea was introduced to the Western world (1660!), although not in the unpredictable teabag form that we see today (a form that has taken much of the fun and excitement out of tea-making, in my humble opinion).

'Sit,' Chase says, and smiles at the waitress, who wears a vintage-style dress and blouse. 'Relax and enjoy the charm of days-gone-by, as it says in the brochure.'

Oh, the *brochure*! I get it. This is a *themed* coffee shop.

'Could I see the brochure, Chase?' I ask. 'I like background information. It's often fascinating, even if badly written.' Once I spent so long reading a brochure at a re-created gold rush town that the place closed before I could see the mine, as it was past the horses' bedtime.

Chase waves my words away. 'I was just speaking about brochures in *general*, George. Because that's what they all say: *enjoy the charm of days-gone-by*. So do it. Without a brochure. I want you to get used to being out of your comfort zone. Because from now on, who knows what will happen?'

Gulp!

I order tea, and just to prove to Chase that I can survive *in* or *out* of my coffee shop comfort zone, I add sugar *and* dunk a biscuit, two things that no Parker person would ever do unless they'd lost their mind and all their teeth at the same time.

Chase checks his phone. 'Clementine is up.' He taps the screen. 'And so is the Australian Stock Exchange.' He shows me a long figure. 'That's the value of my share portfolio. Now for a little internet banking and . . .' His fingers tap-dance. 'There. Two million bucks should do it. We're clear for take-off.'

I can feel my heart beating fast and hard.

'Don't look so worried, George,' Chase says. 'You'll upset the dog. Anyway, I usually find that just as many good things happen as bad things. So we should survive. In the end.'

I suppose that's reassuring.

'Regardless,' Chase continues, 'check this out.' He shows me a photo of an elephant standing in a demolished house. 'Prince Jimahl says there's a big difference between the words *go* and *whoa* as far as elephants are concerned. Luckily, this was the neighbour's place.' Chase shrugs. 'Anyway, I'll get the bill.'

We leave, and on the ground floor, when Amy chases a mouse down its hole, I find a copper coin. It's a King George the Fifth penny, dated 1930. And although I am only an amateur numismatist, I know it's very valuable.

'If we sold this penny,' I tell Chase, 'I could help with our expenses. It's worth . . . a lot.'

Chase grins. 'Keep it for emergencies, George. But now we'd better get back to school to pack. Clementine sent me a flight plan. She wants to leave at about fifteen- or sixteen-hundred hours-*ish*, tomorrow or the day after tomorrow-*ish*, kind of thing.'

'That's rather imprecise, isn't it, Chase?' I say. 'For an international flight.'

'You think so?' Chase shrugs. 'Whatever. Anyway, Clemmy's quite superstitious. So we have to fit in with that, too. She won't take off if a black cat crosses the runway. Or a white horse. She's got all the knowledge in the world about that sort of thing.'

I'm not sure I'd call it *knowledge*, but I keep quiet.

'I look forward to meeting her,' I say.

Chase nods. 'You should. She was runner-up in the Miss Universe contest and invented an incredibly accurate tracking device for rock formations and iron ore mines.'

'But those things don't move, Chase.'

'I didn't say it was a *useful* invention,' Chase answers. 'I just said it was accurate. Now come on. Let's go.'

I do as Chase suggests, and as we head back to school, I must say today has been some day.

And tomorrow's still to come!

CHAPTER SEVEN

While Chase attends to the paperwork with the headmaster, I pack my tartan suitcase. This takes three minutes, as I don't have much stuff. Amy pays close attention as her bowl, lead, and jacket go in. Next to my bed, there's a box lined with my spare towel for her to sleep on, reminding me how strange it is to have another living thing in my room. I mean, *books are the loveliest and liveliest of companions*, as my mother says, but they're a bit limited after they've been read.

I look out my window, feeling fresh in my environmentally approved organically grown hemp and flax pyjamas. Amy stands on a chair, her front paws on the sill. Tapley Grammar is spread out below, soft-edged in the dusk. It's an amazing place, but there are other amazing places in the world, I'm sure. I consult my watch. Eight thirty p.m. Not so bad; only an hour and a half past my normal bedtime.

'Time to hit the sack,' I tell Amy. 'We've got a big day tomorrow.' And into our respective beds we hop.

I look down. Two bright black eyes look up, and I can hear one short tail tapping on cardboard. The sound makes me smile. My world feels somehow bigger. Better. And brighter.

Following a five-minute interview with the headmaster that went surprisingly smoothly, Chase and I pull our suitcases towards the school gates. Amy is in my backpack, her head sticking out, forcing me to tell Brigadier Roylance, the senior gardener, that she is a bobble-headed toy destined for the back shelf of my father's Rolls Royce.

'Good show,' says Brigadier Roylance. 'Carry on, lads. And if you see any enemy troops, you have my permission to shoot to kill. Cheerio.'

Chase and I walk to the Tapley Grammar bus stop that sits under an old oak tree.

'Does your father really have a Rolls Royce?' Chase asks.

'No, he has a fold-up commuter bicycle.' I watch Amy looking into a hollow in the tree. 'I don't like to fib, Chase. But I had to protect Amy.'

'Yes,' Chase replies, 'generally it's best to play a straight bat. But when lives are at stake, you can be a little inventive with the truth. Because the world does move in *strange* ways.'

I can't argue with that, because suddenly something spotted and possum-like shoots out of the hollow and climbs up into the oak's highest branches.

'That's an odd-looking cat,' Chase says. 'Wee-*erd*.'

'It's not a cat,' I say disbelievingly. 'It's a spotted-tail quoll. They're virtually extinct around here, Chase. Until now.'

Chase takes out his phone and photographs the quoll.

'Well, that's one semi-extinct animal we've brought back to life, George,' he says with satisfaction. 'Very good. Anyway, here's the bus.'

We sit up the back of the bus, where I've never sat before, as my mother has warned me that it's where hooligans, hoodlums, swearers, and low-pants wearers like to be. But it seems relatively safe, because Chase and I are the only ones here.

'There must be *more* than one quoll,' I say to Chase. 'For there to be *one* quoll. Reproductively speaking.' I blush. 'If you follow me.'

'You *old devil*, George!' Chase whacks me. 'You and your *reproductively* speaking. Wow. You're a firecracker! You'll be talking about reproductive *organs* shortly! Boy, you're really off the leash now!' Chase leans comfortably in the corner. 'Say, Parkie. Does this bus driver remind you of anyone . . . *famous*?'

The lady driver wears a peaked cap, a tight green jacket, and has long blonde hair. As I've been busy working on a simplified counting system that uses fewer numbers but includes half the letters of the Greek alphabet, I don't watch much TV.

'Does she sell used cars?' I ask.

Chase laughs. 'No, you goose. I think she might be a rockstar. First name starts with K. Second begins with M.'

It's not Dolly Parton or Miss Piggy, then. I put on my glasses and sneak a peek.

'Nope,' I say. 'Nothing there for me, I'm afraid, Chase. I'm not very good with popstars.'

'No kidding?' Chase digs in a pocket and hands me a business card.

Chase Landon-Bond: a can-do type of guy in a go-to type of situation.

'When we get off, George,' he instructs, 'ask for her autograph. And we'll see what we get.' He hands me a solid gold pen inscribed with the words, *Happy Third Birthday, Chase.*

When we pull into Lonsdale railway station, I

politely ask the driver for her autograph. She smiles, asks me my name, and writes on the card, and I thank her. Her sequinned jacket does seem rather low-cut and *frilly*, I think, for a bus driver.

'What does it say, George?' Chase enquires.

'*Dear George*,' I read out loud, '*be kind and look after your dog. Signed, Kylie M*.' I shake my head. 'We're no further ahead than we were fifteen minutes ago, Chase.'

Chase blows out a breath. 'Boy, Georgie-boy, for a really smart kid, you're on a learning curve about as steep as the Empire State Building. Still, let's grab our tickets. Train's due in five.'

We go into the old station. It has a high roof designed to allow smoke from the steam engines to escape – a good idea, quite obviously, otherwise the carbon monoxide would suffocate the people waiting below.

'Train,' announces Chase, getting up. 'The old red rattler has arrived.'

We find seats on the train and I open my backpack a little so Amy can poke her head out.

'Chase,' I say. 'Why are we going to New York?'

'Oh, we might take in a concert at Madison Square Garden,' he answers casually. 'Then we'll get onto our rescue mission.'

Rescue mission? 'And what might our *rescue mission* be, Chase?' I am now officially worried.

'At this point, George,' Chase says, 'the less you know the better. Let me just say that your expertise will help us liberate someone from somewhere rather high that also has rather high security. And then we have to get us and that someone out of that country and back to where we started.'

Now I'm truly alarmed.

'I don't have any *expertise*, Chase,' I say. 'I'm only good in theory. Once my mother had to call the fire brigade when I got a finger stuck wrapping a Christmas present. I was holding the knot, then everything went black. You see? Useless.'

Chase pats Amy. 'You're not useless, George. You're *useful*. You're just going to have to *stretch* yourself.'

Stretch myself? Holy smoke.

'Well, Chase.' I take a long breath. 'I'll do my best.'

Chase nods. 'I know you will.' We gather our stuff as the train glides into Southern Cross station. 'Your talent as a master of disguise and your acting ability will come in handy.'

I follow Chase out of the train and onto the platform.

'I have very little acting ability,' I say. 'And I'm no *master* of disguise, Chase. I am nothing and no one *but* George Errol Erling Edron Parker.'

Chase hardly listens. 'That's exactly why you *can* be a master of disguise,' he says. 'Because you're a blank canvas, George. No one *ever* notices you. Which will allow us to get into places where people wouldn't want us to be, and get out again – alive.'

Good golly! That sounds not only somewhat insulting but incredibly dangerous. Chase gives me a winning smile, which he's good at, because he wins lots of things.

'Chill, Georgie-boy.' He sets off up the platform, dragging his case. 'Don't worry. I'll make sure you practise before we tackle the *big* one.'

Oh, dear.

CHAPTER EIGHT

Chase's house is huge, and has a tower, a long driveway, a beautiful garden, and a honey-coloured cow looking at us over a fence. My little brick house would fit in the letterbox.

'Where do your parents live, George?' Chase shuts the gates.

'Near Melbourne University,' I say, as we walk up the drive. 'Behind the Research Centre for Hopefully Useful Scientific Programs, where they work. What do your parents do, Chase?'

'My mother designs extremely overpriced hats and clothes,' Chase tells me. 'And my dad runs an international hedge fund.'

I know what a hat is, but I have no clue about an international hedge fund — although I bet it has nothing to do with hedges.

'It's an investment thing,' Chase explains, 'that uses other people's money. The idea is to make as many hundreds of millions of bucks as quickly as possible without screwing the world economy. But sometimes that just happens. Then you start all over again. With someone else's money. It's a lot of fun when it goes right.'

'Golly,' I say. 'Anyway, will your parents mind my being here?'

'No.' We climb the front steps. Chase takes a key out from under the doormat. 'They've actually gone into hiding, because there's a little problem with the hedge fund's money. Which happens now and then.'

Chase's life seems very exciting compared to mine. All I do is get up, use the appropriate face washer, fold and box my pyjamas, write some maths poetry, think about chess, go to school, eat tea, look at the stars, then sleep.

'Harriet the housekeeper will make dinner,' Chase says. 'And we'll go up into the tower. It helps to think when you have a decent view.'

I see a flag flying from the tower. It's pink and features a black skull-and-crossbones with gold dollar signs for eyes.

'My mum designed that flag,' Chase explains. 'She felt the last one wasn't politically correct.'

'What was the last one?' I feel it would have had to have been pretty bad if this one is better.

'A picture of my great-grandfather shooting a unicorn.' Chase opens the door. A five-metre-wide stairway leads upwards. 'I'm going to change the culture of this family, George,' he adds. 'I'm sick of people trying to hijack the private jet. Or asking for their diamonds back when we no longer have them. I'll be wanting your input.'

Oh, dear. As I've said before, neither input nor output are my strong points. I follow Chase into a room bursting with flowers.

'My mother has the flowers flown in,' Chase explains. 'Even when no one's home.'

Chase takes a green bottle from a silver ice-bucket.

'Non-alcoholic champagne, George.' He pops the cork. 'We have it made in France for occasions that aren't that special. Care for a flute?'

I nod, even though it worries me how the bubbles might leave my body after they've gone into it. Chase pours us a glass each.

'Cheers.' We tap glasses. 'To us and our mission. Let's hope it doesn't end in total disaster.'

I certainly agree with that. 'Chase,' I say timidly, 'if you want to do the right thing, why don't you cancel the flowers when your mum's away? Then you could sponsor a child in a poor country. It's like five dollars a week. It would be win–win.'

'Good thinking.' Chase opens his phone, Googles something and sends a text, then looks at me. 'Now, one kid for five dollars, Parkie. How many kids for five hundred and fifty dollars?'

'One hundred and ten,' I answer.

'I'll take two hundred.' Chase hits buttons then pockets his phone. 'Done. Right. To the tower. We've got things to consider. Very serious things.'

The view from the tower is amazing. Below us, Melbourne spreads in all directions.

'I have a twin sister,' says Chase. 'Isobel. She hit her head in a mystery ice-skating accident at a nine-star Alaskan wilderness lodge last year. She's always been incredibly intelligent, but since then, no one can work out if she's still smart because she's only said three words in the last twelve months. She's in an institution in New York City, which is where you come in, George.'

'I'd prefer not to be put into an institution, Chase,' I say. 'If you don't mind.'

Chase puts his feet up on a velvet stool.

'Negative to that,' he replies. 'The idea is that because you're also *extremely* intelligent, George, you can work out if her memory can be recovered. And if that's your *diagnosis*, then we'll rescue her.'

'Chase,' I say desperately, 'I'm not a doctor. I can't diagnose anyone.'

'No,' Chase agrees. 'But you're a fast learner. *Apparently*. So I've ordered a pile of medical books for you to study on the jet.'

I feel like I'm trapped on a runaway train that's speeding towards a bridge built by delinquent teenagers who have no mechanical aptitude or understanding of gravity.

'We leave tomorrow,' Chase says. 'Do you think you'll need a stethoscope? No need to think about operating quite yet. You might have to work up to that.'

'Perhaps, Chase,' I stammer, 'we'll wait and see what medical supplies I'll need. What will we do with Amy, by the way?'

Chase looks puzzled. 'Take her with us, of course. Animals can be very helpful in the treatment of all sorts of illness.'

I do know that. It's just that taking a pet across the world isn't generally allowed.

'By the way,' Chase adds. 'The last words Isobel said were, *Ursus arctos horribilis*! Her team of neurophysiologists says she's speaking rubbish. Those words, George? Mean anything to you?'

'It's the scientific name of the grizzly bear,' I answer. 'Who *doesn't* know that?'

Chase laughs. 'I knew it!' He pours me another drink. 'You're the *man*, GP!'

That night, lying in a massive bed, I feel lonely. If not for Amy wagging her tail against the side of a non-alcoholic champagne box, I'd even consider myself unhappy. But then I think of Isobel, perhaps locked in a room with bars on the window, in a strange city, alone and a long way from home.

Maybe I *might* be able to help her?

After all, I did assist Chase in sponsoring those two hundred African kids, and that was a good thing.

'Well done, George,' I whisper to myself. 'Well done.'

CHAPTER NINE

Early the next morning, I go downstairs with Amy. I can hear pots clanging in the kitchen, so I knock on the door and Harriet the housekeeper appears.

'Oh, good morning, Master George.' Harriet is dressed in black, apart from a white baseball cap. 'You're a little early for brunch. Why don't you take Miss Amy for a walk in the garden?'

'Please don't call me Master George, Harriet,' I say. 'Just George would be fine.'

'Just George?' Harriet holds up a finger. 'Or is that *just* George? Or is that just Just George?'

'George,' I say, and head for the front door. 'Thank you!' Then we are outside in the cool air and it is a great relief.

Twenty minutes later, I see an old red VW Beetle grinding up the hill. It has the numberplate

CLMNTN, and is being driven by a blonde woman in a pilot's uniform. She waves and I wave back. Then I see Harriet the housekeeper standing on the front steps. She has a megaphone.

'Attention, Just George!'

Oh, here we go. So I stand to attention, Tapley-style, as that's what we do before the nightly stock market report. Then I wonder if Harriet means that I should *pay* attention?

'At ease, Just George!'

I relax.

'Brunch will be served in the conservatorium, Just George! Please keep the doors shut! Or the butterflies will escape! Over!'

Butterflies?

'Over,' I call back. 'Thank you, Harriet.'

'Thank you, Just George! Over!'

Harriet takes Amy and me into a domed glass room that is filled with tropical plants and blue and purple butterflies. I see there is a table set for four, one chair higher than the rest.

'The high chair is for Miss Amy,' Harriet says. 'How does she like her eggs?'

'I don't know that she likes eggs, Harriet.' I see Amy has her paws up on the glass; she seems to like the butterflies, though.

From behind a fern, Clementine appears.

'Hi, I'm Clemmy.' She smiles so brightly that I take a step back. 'I'll be your pilot today. Estimated flying time to New York is – oh, well, a fair while.' She shrugs. 'I'm sure we'll get there in the end.' Again she smiles. 'That autopilot is a lot of fun. If you get it right.'

'I'm George,' I stammer. 'And this is Amy.' I see Amy has what looks like a bright blue tissue in her mouth. 'And that used to be a blue morpho butterfly,' I add. 'Scientific name, *Morpho peleides*. From the Amazon rainforest.'

'Not any more, it isn't,' Clementine says cheerfully. 'Let's sit, George. I'm famished. I just did a swimsuit commercial. For Chase's mother's fashion label. It's called "Expensively Topless".'

'Oh, really?' I look down at the tablecloth. 'Um, how creative.'

Chase walks into the conservatorium. He's wearing a shirt that is about the same colour that the butterfly used to be, kind of a rare azure blue.

'The medical books are on the jet, George.' Chase

joins us at the table. 'Hi, Clemmy. How did the commercial go?'

'Fantastic.' She smiles, her teeth so white and her eyes so green that I wonder if she's an alien. 'The advertising agency has come up with a new slogan for the entire worldwide campaign. It's "*Go Expensively Topless*"!'

I wait to see if there's any more to the slogan, but that appears to be it. I look at Chase, to see what he thinks of this masterpiece of marketing genius.

'Incredible.' Chase unfolds his napkin. 'Eat up now, George. We've got a huge day ahead. I recommend the Swedish pancakes with aged Canadian maple syrup. All to be washed down with chilled milk from our very own cow, Priscilla, whom you met yesterday.'

'Who milked the cow, Chase?' It can't have been Harriet – she'd never get past the cow's name to get started down the other end.

'Miss Miriam,' Chase says. 'Here she is now.'

A big girl with rosy cheeks carries in a large blue jug of milk. She also wears yellow wooden clogs.

'Um, good morning, Miss Miriam,' I say, as she fills my glass.

'Miss Miriam's English isn't up to much,' Chase explains. 'She's Dutch. She's settled in nicely, though her shoes are a bit rackety, being wooden. But she'll be fine if she keeps to the carpet.'

'Thank you, Miriam,' I say. 'I believe the Dutch dairy industry is a world-leader for automatic udder sanitation and microchip herd management processes.'

'Oh, *ja*!' Miriam smiles almost as brightly as Clementine. 'Cow udders! You would not believe!'

That's confusing, so I simply smile until she leaves.

'I've submitted the flight plan, Chase.' Clementine shuts her laptop. 'Refuel in Hawaii and LA. Arrive JFK at NYC in the p.m. in time for dinner, Friday. Or thereabouts.'

Chase lifts his glass of milk. 'Well, good luck to us. This is going to be wild. Next stop, the United States of America!'

We clink glasses, as I don't think I have any choice.

'Well, hopefully.' Clemmy smiles that killer smile. 'Anyway, it's a big country, America. You'd have to be unlucky to miss it completely.'

CHAPTER TEN

Clemmy drives us out to the airport, the VW Beetle fully loaded. Amy sits on top of our bags, panting happily.

'Are you sure American Customs, or Homeland Security, won't put Amy in quarantine, Chase?' I ask. 'She might be there for months. Or worse.'

'Of course they won't,' Chase says. 'Prince Jimahl once took a pygmy hippopotamus to Miami. Everyone loved it. They thought it was a Shetland pony.'

Clementine doesn't turn in to the airport carpark but into a place called 'Trusty Garry's Totally Used Cars'.

'What we do when we fly,' Chase explains, 'is drop the car off and Garry sells it. Then when we come back, he sells us another to go home in. Saves time and effort.'

I don't mean to be critical, but this sounds *ridiculous*.

'Yes, Chase,' I say, 'but that must *cost* heaps.'

Clemmy stops in front of a little tin office. Out

comes a man wearing purple shorts, a sea captain's hat, and a yellow Hawaiian shirt.

'What's your point here, George?' Chase looks at me. 'If you don't mind me asking.'

'Well,' I say, 'if you park the car at the airport, you can drive home in it. You'll save thousands of dollars. Then you could, say, sponsor an endangered tiger with the money.'

'Sponsor a tiger?' Chase appears thoughtful. 'I'd prefer to adopt one, Parkie. And keep it at home. Can you do that?'

'I don't think so. Sponsoring is the way to go, Chase. Generally.'

Chase turns to Clementine. 'Let's do what George says.' He winds down the window. 'Sorry, Trusty Garry. We're going to park the car and sponsor a tiger. Catch ya later.'

'Good thinking!' Trusty Garry gives us a salute. 'Make sure you get a stripy one! The other ones are lions!'

'What we *could* do, George,' Chase says, 'is get our two hundred sponsored kids to *visit* the tiger. I'm sure they'd all be thrilled to bits.'

'Er, tigers are in India,' I explain. 'The children are in Africa.'

'Really?' Chase takes off his safety belt. 'When did that happen? Whatever, let's get to the jet. And George, you play the piano, don't you? Because there's one on the plane.'

I can play the piano, but it must cost a *fortune* to carry a piano in a private jet.

'If we . . . off-loaded the piano, Chase,' I say carefully, 'we'd save thousands in jet fuel. We could then sponsor a whole family of endangered orang-utans in Borneo.'

'Well, I do like those o-rangas,' Chase says. 'But man, watching them eat a banana is like watching paint dry. *Speed* it up, guys!'

Clemmy signals with a finger. 'Why don't we *give* the piano *to* the o-rangas? I'm sure one of the really bright ones could pick it up in a couple of days. It might take their minds off things.'

'It . . . might,' I say. 'But it would be more efficient to off-load the piano *here*. And simply send the money to save the orang-utans over *there*.'

'Yes, that might be smart,' says Chase. 'But first, let's go to the private gate and get on the jet. And you'll still have time for a few tunes before take-off, George. Which might influence my decision one way or the other.'

Chase's phone dings. 'Good news, Parkie.' He high-fives me, my first ever. 'We've won a gold cup for sponsoring the most kids in Africa in one day. Boy, Mum'll be thrilled. She can put flowers in it.'

I know it's rude to be telling Chase what he should do with money, but really, it's simply changing one type of wealth into another. It's win-win! Maybe I'll succeed at Tapley, after all!

Then we are on the amazingly comfortable jet.

'Have you got your rabbits' feet?' Chase asks Clemmy, who's fixing her make-up in the cockpit mirror.

'Yep.' She holds up a furry handful. 'We'll be right to go as soon as I can find the keys.'

'No worries,' says Chase. 'They're probably in your handbag or under the seat.' He points at the piano. 'Go on, Georgie. Play.'

So I strap myself into the piano and play 'Old Man Emu', 'I Still Call Australia Home', and finish with a toe-tapping Christmas carol or two.

'You're right,' says Chase, when I finish. 'We can do without that thing. I'll call the guys to come and get it. You can eBay it.'

Then, minus the piano, we are streaking high into the bright blue western sky.

'Oops.' Clementine speaks over the intercom. 'You said America, didn't you, Chase? Not Adelaide?'

Chase presses a button. 'Yes, America, Clemmy. The big one. Aim for the north-eastern bit. That's where New York is.'

With that, Clemmy pulls the jet into a screaming U-turn, and our faces stretch like rubber.

'Thanks, Chase,' I say, when we level out. 'For everything.'

'Don't mention it, dude.' Chase brings up a photograph of a tall building on his personal seat screen. 'That's the John J Hospital hospital in New York, where Isobel is.' He glances at me. 'Correction. That's the John J Hospital hospital that we're going to get Isobel *out* of.'

'It seems to have rather tight security,' I say worriedly, seeing armed guards at the front doors and video surveillance cameras all over the place.

Chase stares at the picture. 'Ever seen *Spiderman*, the movie?'

I gulp. 'Er, no, Chase. I'm more of a documentary type of guy. Did you know that sea otters actually use a stone to break open shells and—'

'Well,' Chase says, somewhat rudely, 'the Spider-man method won't work then. We'll have to work out something else, possibly more dangerous. On another subject, have you been to Paris?' Chase hands me one of the monster muffins Harriet baked. 'Isobel loves the old book stalls by the river. Last time, she bought a collector's edition of *Harry Potter and the Big Croissant* and a thirty-metre river barge.'

A *river barge*?

'Er, what did she do with the barge?' I ask politely.

Chase brings up a photo of a massive black steel boat called the *Solange*.

'She had it re-fitted and redecorated and parked it in town,' he informs me. 'Which might come in handy if we end up in France.'

France? Since when did France become part of the plan? Because, as my dad says, *Parkers always plan to have a plan already planned. Or that's the plan.* Well, I don't see any sign of a plan here, that's for sure.

Chase settles back in his seat. 'As my dad says, George, only plonkers plan plans because plans are for plonkers.'

Well, I don't know about that!

CHAPTER ELEVEN

We fly on, land in Honolulu, refuel, and take off.

'Normally, Georgie-boy,' Chase says, 'I would've stayed in Hawaii so you could've surfed Pipeline. It's a massively dangerous wave and you would've loved it. But we're in a hurry.'

Me? Surf? All I do on the beach is follow the shade of the umbrella like a human sundial and work on my design for a sun-smart seven-piece bikini.

'I'm not the beach, er, beach bottom type, Chase. I'm rather too pale.'

'You're only pale,' Chase says, 'because you live like a mushroom. You won't know yourself if we ever get back to Australia. Truly.'

If?

What!?

'I'd rather like,' I mumble, 'to be back for first term, Chase. For one thing – well, two things, really – my mother has already bought my new school shoes, and if I'm late, I might have grown out of them.

Parker people pride themselves on forward-thinking footwear purchases, Chase. We don't just walk in and walk out of the shop with a new pair of shoes, no sir.'

Chase laughs and lifts a hank of my hair.

'What d'you care about school *shoe* selection, Geepy? When you've gone and got yourself a *haircut* like this?'

'The haircut was an accident, Chase.' I wonder if he'll now kick me off the plane with or without a parachute. 'The hair salon caught fire when I was halfway through my double-shot short-back-and-sides, and we had to evacuate.'

'An accident? Really?' Chase looks disappointed. 'Well, that's okay. You've done some good things already. You have up-side, George, as they say at school. Although they've never said that to you personally.'

That's true. No one has ever said I've got up-side, although I must have some, because everyone does.

'I used to think you were extremely ordinary,' Chase adds. 'Now I think you might be the one and only *extraordinary* DeeJay G-Pak.'

It takes me a while to work out that *I'm* DeeJay G-Pak.

Chase flips off his seatbelt. 'Now, do you want to fly this plane or not?'

'I can't fly a jet, Chase!' My heart smacks hard in my chest. 'No one in my family can drive a car. I can't even ride a bike.'

Chase stands. 'Oh, give it a whirl. There's nothing up here to hit. Besides, I can wake Clementine if there's a mechanical failure.'

Five minutes later, I'm wearing a headset and flying a Gulfstream 460 at nine hundred kilometres an hour. Clemmy sits next to me, bare feet up on the dashboard, painting her toenails.

'George,' she says, 'don't fly into that really massive – whoops! Too late.'

The jet drops like a rock, lightning flashes, and we go into a vertical nose dive. I've flown *right* into the black heart of a supercell thunderstorm!

Clemmy screws the lid back on her toenail polish and puts her feet down.

'Pull up and go left, George, when you're ready, as we're due to hit the ocean in eleven seconds. Make that eight.'

I do what Clemmy says, and suddenly, like a rocket, we're flying in clear air again. Oh my golly gosh, that was horrible!

'Do you want to have a shot at landing in Los Angeles?' Clementine asks. 'That'd be something funny for Show and Tell.'

'N-n-n-o thanks,' I stammer, then hand over the controls and wobble back to my seat.

Chase opens his laptop. 'Hmmm. Bit of bad news, Parks.' He pulls a face. 'My dad says the dear old hedge fund has hit a slight speed bump and lost two hundred million dollars. Which some people want back. Kind of desperately.'

'Two hundred *million*, Chase,' I say. 'Where's it gone?'

Chase shrugs. 'Down the gurgler, I guess.' He fastens his seatbelt. 'Strap yourself in, GP, I think we're in for a rough ride. Better stay on the plane in LA,' he adds. 'These people will be coming after us. And I don't want any of us photographed, shot, or kidnapped.'

That makes two of us, at least.

'Now, George,' Chase adds, 'pick a few shares on the stock market. Shares that will go up – a lot. Unless your parents can send us a couple of hundred million they have lying about? Plus another fifty for good luck, because that seems to have wandered off as well.'

'My parents are *research* scientists, Chase. They're really smart but they're really poor.'

'Pardon me for saying this, Parkie,' Chase replies. 'If they were really smart, they wouldn't be really poor. You have to turn that ship around. Because someone is going to have to cough up a fair few million somehow, some way, and soon. D'you have any pets, George?'

'Only Amy.'

Chase glances at Amy, who is watching *101 Dalmations* on her personal, dog-friendly seat screen. Then Chase looks at me.

'I don't have to spell this out to you, Parkie, but I will. D-E-A-D D-O-G. These people will come after us and everything we've got to get that money. And leave no survivors. And on another subject,' Chase adds, 'you'd better put those medical books in the overhead locker or under the seat in front, because it'd be kinda dumb to get killed by one if we have a rough landing.'

I push the pile of books under the seat. Yes, it'd be rather a sick joke, so to speak, to have my skull fractured by a six-hundred-page book about the human brain and how to keep it in good condition.

We land at LA International Airport to refuel.

'So what do your parents actually *do*?' Chase asks, bouncing a ball for Amy, who jumps at it like a trout after a bug.

'They're studying space rocks for possible uses on Earth,' I say. 'But as an experiment, my dad and I have a backyard project growing algae for bio-fuel. It could be worth millions. But at the moment, it's just smelly green weedy stuff in a pond.'

Clementine's voice comes over the intercom. 'Hold onto your hats, kids. It's time for take-off. We have bad guys incoming.'

I look out and see three men in black suits and sunglasses running towards the plane. Then our twin jet engines scream and we blast off like a Phantom fighter leaving an aircraft carrier. Luckily I have a good hold of Amy and had visited the bathroom three minutes earlier.

'Next stop, New York,' Chase says. 'If you can make it there, GP, you can make it anywhere.'

Make what? A last wish?

'Um, any sign of that money, yet?' I ask Chase.

Chase blows out a breath. 'Nope. But Dad put fifty million in my account for safekeeping.' Chase brings up a chart of the New York Stock Exchange.

'So basically, GP, you and I've got to invest it. Which means you have to use your super brain to work out what we'll invest it *in*.'

Me? Invest *fifty* million dollars? That's mad!

'My dad says education is the best investment in the world,' I volunteer.

'Get real, George.' Chase taps my head with a spoon, as if it is a boiled egg. 'And get cracking. Because it's my parents' money paying for your scholarship. Or it was. So if we want to go back to good old Tapley Grammar, I suggest you come up with something brilliant.'

'Oh,' I say, 'dear.'

'Don't do the *oh dear* thing.' Chase brings up a phone app with a smiley horse icon. 'What do you know about racehorses, George? Do your parents have any? At all?'

No Parker would ever, or *could* ever, own a racehorse.

'No,' I say. 'But I understand the theory of trying to pick a winner. Why?'

Chase's phone screen fills with numbers and names.

'International form guide,' he explains. 'They're racing at Ascot in England. I'm thinking of putting twenty million bucks on Limpy Prince in the fourth.

I like the sound of him. He's a teenaged horse whose mother is Home At Last and his dad is King Swampy Slow Coach.'

'Don't do it, Chase,' I say. 'Why don't we put that fifty million in the international overnight money market? We'll earn interest and we can't lose it. Then if we see other opportunities, we'll have the money. Plus extra.'

Chase considers this as we fly over the American Midwest, where you'll find the Corn Palace, a magnificent building decorated all over with corn, a place that's on my bucket list to visit before I die, as visiting it after I die would be hard to arrange, and not much fun for anyone, ha ha!

'Good thinking, GP.' Chase hands across his laptop. 'Talk to our banking guy in Geneva, Mr X. The password is HELLO.'

I type and suddenly the image of a big man in a dark room comes up.

'What language does he speak?' I ask.

'He doesn't,' Chase says. 'Just type, and Bob's your uncle.'

I do that then log off. Clemmy's voice comes over the intercom.

'Landing in New York pretty soon, guys. Ground

66

temperature, well, a bit on the cold side. And there's some of that what-do-you-call-it? That fluffy stuff. Snow.'

Chase pushes his intercom button. 'Great, Clemmy. You're always so accurate.'

Really? Way below, the landscape is blanketed in white. It's beautiful.

'The land of *opportunity*,' I say. 'America.'

'*Every* land is the land of opportunity,' Chase says. 'Speaking of which, what are you like at writing pop songs? Those things can earn millions overnight.'

Me? 'Well, I do like an old-fashioned bush ballad or a fun-filled folk song,' I say. 'You know, something about shearing angry sheep or straightening old nails, and so forth. They don't write songs like that anymore.'

'And you'd better not start,' Chase says. 'No, you'll need to write about love. Falling in or out. One way or the other. I don't care. Whatever feels best.'

'I haven't had much experience in those areas, Chase,' I say. 'It's one of my weak points, I suppose.'

Chase swivels in his leather seat. 'Don't be ridiculous. You love Amy. Write about her. No one'll know she's a dog. And I bet you five million bucks that you're in love with that girl, Charlotte, from the jetty. Because she was falling in love with you.' He puts out his hand. 'Come on. Five mill. *Bet!*'

I sit on my hands. 'She wasn't falling in *love* with me,' I say. 'She was *appreciative* that I saved Amy from the deadly grip of the *swirling* sea.'

Chase pokes the limp collar of my Tapley Chargers tournament top, with its energy-saving accordion-type sleeves and onboard bandaid station for blistered fingers.

'There's your first two lines *right* there, George. You can write the rest after you've seen how Beyonce or Rihanna do it at Madison Square Gardens tonight. They're worth *trillions*.'

I haven't heard of them. I'm not even sure if they're people.

'Hold on to your hats!' Clemmy announces. 'We're going in! Don't worry about arming the doors or cross-checking. I never do.'

Out of the window, I can see hundreds of tall buildings and the Statue of Liberty.

'New York!' I say. 'Wow!'

'*That's* the spirit,' says Chase. 'Be optimistic! Because it's more fun, even if things turn out worse than you can ever imagine.'

We land at JFK Airport, Clemmy weaving her way between passenger jets that lumber around like shiny white monsters. I've heard New York is smoggy, but today the sky is an iridescent blue and the snow is dazzling. For a moment, I think of my folks working on the space rocks, even if I think my algae project has more *commercial potential*, as Chase would say. But my parents believe in working for the good of all people, not just themselves.

'We should,' Chase says carefully, 'hide our jet. Otherwise someone we owe money to might try and make it *their* jet.'

'Hide it where?' I can't see any dark alleyways or handy trees, ha ha.

'We're in America,' Chase says. 'The military will have a few strike fighters stashed in a shed somewhere. I'm sure they'll let Clemmy park for a while.'

I'm sure they won't. The American military don't look after stuff for you. They blow it up.

Chase unclips his seatbelt and stretches. 'You see, George, Clemmy was judged as the second *best-* looking civilian in the world. And that opens doors. Hangar doors in this case. See? It's happening already.'

A guy in United States Air Force overalls waves at us with orange ping-pong bats. Then we're inside a huge hangar and Clemmy parks the jet into a space marked 'Visitor', between Lightning A-35 fighter-bomber war planes.

I don't believe this. But as I zip Amy in her bag and check the seat pocket, I do know for sure that things are getting stranger and stranger every day.

CHAPTER TWELVE

We find ourselves on Fourth Avenue in New York City. It's crowded with people and traffic, and the air is freezing. Chase checks his phone as we stand outside a very fancy hotel.

'Five star or six, George?' he asks. 'The Ritz-Carlton is nice. Andre, the manager, could get us front-row seats for tonight's concert. No problem.'

'If people are after you, Chase—'

'After *us*, George,' he says. 'They're not too fussy who they shoot. Anyway, carry on.'

'If people are after *us*,' I say reluctantly, 'we should stay somewhere less obvious than a luxury hotel. And save thousands of dollars into the bargain.'

'Good thinking.' Chase hands me a black leather jacket from his bag. 'Put this on. You're turning blue, and that's not a good look. Unless you're thinking of becoming a whale.'

Chase's jacket fits so well that no matter which way I turn, it's already got there before me.

'Thanks, Chase.' I see my reflection in the window. *Wow*. Scary rock 'n' roll George! 'Does this make me look too threatening, Chase, d'you think?'

Chase doesn't answer; I'm not sure why.

'Okay, an apartment will do,' Chase decides. 'Good thinking.'

And soon we're in a tenth-floor apartment, gazing over a city that supposedly never sleeps, which doesn't sound very healthy, I must say.

'Without Andre the hotel manager,' Chase says, 'we can't get tickets for tonight's show. We'll have to sneak in, which will give you something exciting to write about in your journal.'

Tapley Grammar boys keep a journal to write down their goals in life, the phone numbers of rich girls, and suburbs they'd like to own. But most boys use it to keep track of their gold bullion, helicopters, private islands, diamond mines, and banking passwords written in invisible ink – which is a real time-waster for the Tapley Help Desk. I just write about my life. So far I have two hundred words.

'On second thoughts, George.' Chase looks down at steam rising from grates in the footpath, as if hell is just below. 'We should destroy your journal. In case you, or it, fall into the wrong hands. Unless you feel able to stand up to torture? Then keep it, by all means.'

I feel a shudder of fear, which I once would have recorded in my journal but certainly won't now.

'I'll get it.' I dip into my backpack but my journal's not there! Fear strikes me like a bolt of lightning. How can I tell a torturer anything when I don't *know* anything? They'd keep on going until I ran out of body parts! 'I must've left it or lost it in Australia, Chase. It might've fallen into the wrong hands already!'

'Hmmm.' Chase shrugs. 'Oh, well, it probably doesn't matter so much.' He looks at me. 'No offence, Parkie, but there'll only be George-stuff in it anyway.'

I guess. And every second line is in George Parker Numeric Code, because it makes me laugh to read in numbers.

'I did draw a map of your house, Chase,' I admit, feeling awful. 'But I didn't orientate it to true north. So cartographically speaking, it's a dog's breakfast.'

Chase smiles slowly. 'As I said, it's only got George-stuff in it. But you know what?'

This is an impossible question: what does the *what* mean? So the answer has to be *what*? Which *isn't* an answer, because it's a question, so we're back to where we started.

'No,' I say. 'What?' Immediately, I get a tension headache.

Chase grins. 'That George-stuff might be *exceptional*.'

I suddenly experience this weird feeling that Chase and I are *actually* friends. For a moment, I forget my lost journal and what effects torture might have on my future.

'Thanks, Chase. I appreciate it.'

'No sweat, GP.' Chase nods. 'Now. New subject.' He throws me his phone. 'Bring up the *Wall Street Journal* and pick some shares. We need to make big bucks and we need to make 'em fast.'

I feel a second shudder of fear, because I am not a qualified financial advisor. I do know that the share market can go down like the *Titanic*, but unlike the *Titanic*, it can keep *on* going down.

'No, Chase.' I hand back his phone. 'We'll look for more *secure* opportunities.'

Chase shrugs. 'Okay, Georgie-boy, but you're not here just for your odd looks. Remember Priority Numero Uno is to visit Isobel and work out our rescue plan. But as we've missed visiting hours today, we'll get our strength up with some New York pizza, then we'll gate-crash that rock show for your creative inspiration.'

I'm *not* a gate-crasher. I don't even go to places where I *am* invited, unless it's to receive a book prize or take part in an experimental medical trial.

'Hey, George!' Clemmy yells down from upstairs. 'Do you want a room with a double bed and view? Or the one with a single bed next to the broom closet?'

Me in a *double* bed? I'd have a panic attack. It'd be like sleeping in the middle of the Simpson Desert. *Double* beds are designed for *two* people. And one of them *cannot* be George Parker! I might dream I was *married*! Then what? Well, I'm not sure what, but I'm not going to risk it.

'I'll have the single thanks, Clemmy,' I call back shakily. 'I'm sure the brooms will tidy up after themselves, ha ha.'

Then I have another thought so catastrophic that I have to sit down.

'Chase,' I say. 'This is really, really serious. I've *forgotten* my *pyjamas*.' I remember leaving them in my Portable Pyjama Storage Facility (a non-allergenic scale replica of a space shuttle) under my pillow at Chase's house.

Chase starts laughing, somewhat insensitively, if I may say so.

'Oh, Georgie-boy!' He slaps his knee. 'Guess what? We have fifty million dollars in the bank! We can *buy* some pyjamas!'

I take a deep, calming breath. 'Oh, good.' Perhaps now isn't the time to tell him that they can't be made of synthetic material, and that they must feature a pattern of an endangered animal species to raise my environmental awareness, even when I'm asleep. 'Because, Chase, no pyjamas equals nightmares for George. And that's an equation I want no part in.'

'Oh, boy.' Chase grins. 'We might end up dead down one of my dad's useless oil wells in Tajikistan, but at least we'll die laughing.'

'*You* might,' I say huffily. 'I won't. Not without pyjamas. I'll die of embarrassment.'

'Georgie.' Chase is serious. 'Embarrassed people are liable to let the cat out of the bag. And because we have hundreds of millions of cats in bags, that cannot happen. Okay?'

I understand. 'I still want pyjamas though, Chase.'

'Clemmy'll fix it,' Chase says. 'While we're at the concert. So get *ready to rock and roll!*'

I would if I knew how.

CHAPTER THIRTEEN

Chase and I take a taxi to Madison Square Garden. Tall buildings and traffic hem us in on all sides.

'Where you boys from?' The taxi driver has an unlit cigar in his mouth and an unlit match, which is just asking for trouble. He looks at me in the rear-view mirror. 'You a hippie from San Francisco, man?'

'No, sir,' I say. 'I am a lower secondary school student from Melbourne, Victoria, Australia. But I did once sit next to a cheerful hippie chappie wearing a purple shirt with pineapples and bananas orbiting around an incredibly inaccurate drawing of a bottle-nosed dolphin.'

'You got a hippie haircut, my friend,' the driver drawls. 'One side anyway. Or you a skinhead? You hippie to the left. You a head–bangin' cat to the right!'

'My hairstyle was the result of circumstances beyond my control,' I answer. 'I can assure you, I prefer a more conservative look that reflects my conservative nature.'

'You a *hippie-head*,' the driver says. 'First one I *ever* seen in New York *City*.'

Chase asks the driver to stop. I see a large brightly lit building with long lines of people outside it. The name, *Rhibeeyonceyh*, is spelled out in startlingly bright lights. Something big is happening here. Or it will be soon. I can feel it!

Chase pays the driver, whom I'm glad to get away from, because if that's what harsh interrogation feels like, no wonder it's banned under the Geneva Convention.

'What *is* a skinhead, Chase?' The question has been bothering me. 'Are they dangerous?'

Chase looks at me. 'You've had a very sheltered childhood, haven't you, George?'

We stand on a wide street. It's cold, but people are laughing and shouting. It's kind of thrilling.

'Not particularly,' I say. 'Although I wasn't allowed to go to the letterbox by myself until I was twelve. A sensible precaution, I would've thought.'

'Yeah, *really* sensible,' Chase says, not bothering to join the end of the queue, which worries me because no Parker has *ever* pushed in anywhere. 'Up here, George.' He turns into a dark side street where gigantic trucks are parked. 'Let's make a plan.'

Oh, good. I like plans. And maps, brochures, pamphlets, and instructional leaflets.

'I don't have a pen,' I say. 'Perhaps I could borrow one?'

'You won't need a pen, George.' Chase drags me into a smelly doorway. We crouch down. 'But you will need to be cool and calm. No matter what.'

I nod. 'I'll do my best.' Boy, there are odours here that make me nervous.

'Right.' Chase's eyes shine in the dark. 'How's your dancing?'

Hmmm, the general Parker opinion of dancing is that it's best left to the experts, or idiots with private health insurance.

'I've *seen* quite a lot of dancing,' I say, trying to be helpful. 'I must admit I struggled with the complexities of "Itsy Bitsy Spider", Chase, so perhaps the gentle art of folk dancing might be my thing?'

'Perhaps it might *not*.' Chase takes a deep breath. 'George, you will do *exactly* what I tell you, which will *not* include folk dancing at any point. So let's hope you've got hidden talents. Come on.'

There is a huge man wearing dark glasses standing beside a door with a silver star on it. Chase stops in the shadows.

'We *dance* to the door,' he hisses, 'because we are *dancers*, right? Do everything I do, *except* talk. And keep *on* dancing. No matter *what*!'

This use of *what* is really confusing; it's just so *general*.

'What might the *what* be, Chase?'

Chase grabs my shirt and talks through gritted teeth.

'The *what* could be freaking *anything*! Now get your dancing shoes *on* and let's *go*!'

Suddenly, from inside the building, the loudest music I've ever heard begins. Chase shouts at me.

'We go on the count of *four*! One. Two. Three. *Four!*'

Something peculiar is happening! The music explodes in my brain, my body gets lift-off, and my feet follow! I tap-dance towards the big security guy, trip over but turn it into a somersault (my first ever), then just when I'm about to do a spin, the music stops. But I don't; I *keep on dancing*.

I leap like a tiger, crouch like a frog then strut like Captain Cook arriving in Australia, before doing a dance interpretation of popcorn popping followed by a scene from the ballet *Swan Lake*, which I've never seen, but it seems to have gone well because the big security guy just says, 'You *dancers*! *Always* late! *Get* inside!'

So Chase and I simply waltz straight in through the door and hide behind a big black curtain.

A thought strikes me as we catch our breath.

'What are we here for again, Chase?'

'You're here,' Chase informs me, 'to learn how to become a pop superstar song-writing billionaire. Like Taylor Swift.'

'Like *what*, Chase?'

Chase looks displeased. 'She's not a freakin' *what*, George. She's a damned *who*!'

'Oh,' I say. 'Well. That's nice. What does Tyler do exactly?'

Chase looks *really* annoyed. 'Which *planet* are you—'

The music starts, ka-*boom*, people swirl wildly, the invisible crowd roars, and then the curtain we're hiding behind flies up! Suddenly Chase and I are surrounded by people in shiny black pants and tiny jackets – then I see the crowd, and they're standing, stamping, and cheering!

'Just do what these *dancing* dudes do!' Chase shouts. '*Whatever* that is!'

No time for questions! Up we jump, and stand like statues like everybody else on stage, until something flat taps me on the head. I look up and see a beautiful young woman in pink and silver on a trapeze, and it's her tapping me on the head with her electric-blue shoe. Then she spins to the floor in a tornado of glitter and sequins.

Chase hisses, '*Tops off* and *teeth out*, George!' He turns on an electric grin and points to his now-bare chest. 'This is *showbiz*, boy!'

Normally I would not expose my upper half anywhere but in the shower or on doctor's orders, but I guess I have to help Chase so – *zip*!

The next hour passes in a flash. One minute I'm a bad-tempered lion, the next I'm sailing a silver yacht on a wire high above the stage, and then I'm dodging a ring of flame because I'm not sure if my socks and undies are one hundred per cent fireproof.

'Keep it up, George,' Chase puffs as we pass. 'Listen to the words. That's where the money is.'

Somehow I find myself in the spotlight with the beautiful singer, who's wearing underwear I've only ever seen in a letterbox catalogue, despite our No Junk Mail, It's Annoying And Environmentally Unfriendly, Thank You Very Much And Have A Fun Day Doing Science If You Have Time sticker.

'Whass *up*!' The beautiful star does the splits.

I *get* it! I have to do the *opposite* of what she says, so I do the splits, too.

'Gedd *down*!' She stands up, confusingly, and now stretches one leg straight out on a grand piano. 'And get *jiggy* with it!'

I'm with my mother on this one. No jigging for George.

Instead, I find myself beside the grand piano, turning pretend pages of music as the superstar sings and plays. Then somehow *I'm* sitting at the piano – so I launch into a tune I wrote called 'Extinct Animals Don't Make Good Pets', which confuses the crowd although the message there is pretty clear, I would've thought. And just when I'm about to start 'Stand Up for the Dugong Because They Can't Stand Up for Themselves', Chase drags me violently off the stage.

'We gotta go!' He nods. 'A guy said they're taking

us to Las Vegas as pretend showgirls. And I doubt your parents would approve.'

I guess it doesn't sound *all* that bad, but Chase is probably right. So I zip up his leather jacket and look for the exit – but we never make it. A security man in a leopard–print suit grabs us.

'The boss wants to see ya,' he growls. 'So guess what?'

'I'm sorry, sir,' I say, 'the only answer to that question is a question, isn't it? Because *what* is the wh—'

Chase elbows me. 'Don't *go* there, George.'

Don't go *where*? Well, it turns out that the *where* is a white room with couches, mirrors, flowers, and bottles of *alcohol*.

'If this is prison,' I whisper to Chase, 'it's quite nice, isn't it? But giving alcohol to under-age law-breakers seems rather irresponsible.'

'Take a seat, boys.' The big man blocks the doorway. 'The boss'll be here shortly.'

'I don't like the look of this,' I whisper.

'Shut,' Chase whispers back, 'up.'

The beautiful star appears in a fluffy white dressing gown and slippers like furry dogs. A little old lady comes in with her and pours three cups of tea. Then she adds milk, so bad luck if anyone is dairy-intolerant because the evening is going to be rather gaseous from now on. The singer sits back, crosses her legs, and looks at me.

'Who designed your leather jacket, darling?'

Is this a trick question?

'Er, pass,' I say.

'My mother,' Chase answers. 'And her company made it.'

'Get the details, Flora,' the superstar says to the little lady. 'We'll buy everything.'

Well, I guess that's a good start, so I sit up straight with my knuckles on my knees to show that I'm both attentive and polite.

'Relax, George,' Chase whispers. 'You look like a startled kangaroo.'

'George,' says the beautiful star. 'You're a dancer, a choreographer, a hair-styling trendsetter, and a musician. Do you feel you could live in Hollywood as a creative consultant? Flora would attend to your every need.'

I try not to look alarmed.

'It would be better if George phones it in from offshore,' Chase says, 'because he prefers *silence* to speaking.' He glares at me. 'He also worships every *single* thing you've ever done. And attends church every day and has eighty million friends on Facebook.'

What's Facebook, I wonder?

The beautiful star glows at me. I try to glow back.

'You're very sweet, George,' she says. 'We'll be in touch. Flora, get George's contacts.'

Then the superstar is gone, and suddenly Chase and I are outside the steel door we came in. A black limousine pulls up silently like a ghost ship and a window whirrs down.

'I can go as far as the Canadian border,' the driver says. 'Or Mexico to the south.'

'It's fine, thanks,' Chase says, as we get into the rear seat. 'We only want to go to Fourth Avenue. So, Georgie, I think we made significant progress.' He sinks back. 'It's time to *relax*.'

'I cannot *begin* to relax,' I answer, 'without pyjamas. I'd rather *die!*'

'Settle down, you ninny.' Chase checks his phone. 'Clemmy's bought you two pairs.'

Two? Generally we only buy one of anything in case I grow, or – rather more unlikely – I shrink.

'Thank goodness.' I unwind a little. 'All I'll need now is a permanent marker to draw an endangered species or two on them, Chase. Or I won't be able to sleep a wink.'

Chase peers at me. 'You're not exactly mainstream are you, George? You certainly are a little bit *out* there.'

Me? The only edge of the envelope I would push, as the saying goes, is the one you press down to seal the thing.

'Positive pyjama illustration,' I say, 'is hardly *non*-mainstream. Not amongst my crowd, anyway. I'll simply draw a pair of dim-witted western swamp tortoises using my kneecaps as templates. And pretty soon you'll see numbers of those short-sighted little fellows crossing the Great Northern Freeway again. Which, come to think of it, could explain the difficult position of survival they find themselves in today.'

Chase has no answer to that.

Just as I thought.

CHAPTER FOURTEEN

I sleep well in my dim-witted western swamp tortoise pyjamas and join Chase at the kitchen table for a morning meeting.

'First, the bad news,' he says. 'My fifty million dollars has been frozen by the people chasing Dad's money, because they think it's *their* money. So we have very little cash for anything.'

'I have eighteen dollars in my purse.' Clemmy applies lipstick, holding a small mirror. 'But I'm shooting a toothpaste commercial this morning, so I'll ask them for an advance.'

'I've got twenty Australian dollars,' I offer. 'So if you two like rolled oats for porridge, we'd be right for a month at least.'

'Save it, Georgie.' Chase taps a finger on the table. 'This afternoon you and I visit Isobel in hospital. How's your medical knowledge coming on? I'll need a diagnosis and prognosis for the next critical phase of Operation Isobel.'

Operation? 'Those neurosurgery books are big,' I explain. 'I'm only halfway through the third, Chase. If I were to operate, I'd really be just blundering around in the dark.'

Chase leans forward. '*Operation*, George, as in what we intend to do regarding the *entire* Isobel situation. Not *operation* as in I want you to poke *anyone* with a scalpel.'

That's a relief!

'So,' Chase slaps the table, 'let's go out for breakfast!'

'But rolled oats are—'

'*Disgusting*,' Chase says. 'No, we're going to an American *diner*. Let's hit the trail.'

'One problem.' I circle a finger. 'Those rotating stools could go very wrong for me.'

Chase stops mid-step. 'George,' he says, lowering his foot. 'I've just re-wound time so I cannot hear what you said, okay?'

What?

Now Chase has got me doing the damn *what* thing!

'Pardon me, Chase.' I *am* a little angry. 'If you think the danger of rotating stools is ridiculous, then *your* whacky statement about reversing *time* is a slap in the face to quantum physicists worldwide! With that kind of nutty talk, you'll only end up looking like a crackpot. And that is a situation I have so far successfully avoided in my short but uneventful life!'

Chase and I go to a noisy Manhattan diner called the Stackery. Upon entering, I smartly select a red vinyl booth and a waitress appears. She's chewing gum or tobacco and has a rose tattoo on her arm, which looks somewhat botanically incorrect. Above her elbow, an anchor floats in mid-air, which just makes no sense at all.

'Pancakes and maple syrup, George.' Chase shuts the menu. 'Let's do it. Big stacks and big coffees all round, thank you, madam.'

'I'm not sure about coff—' Before I can explain my total lack of experience drinking coffee, the waitress leaves. Chase shrugs.

'This is New York, GP. We'll need kilojoules and caffeine. Now here's the plan. We eat, we go back to the apartment, have lunch, then visit Isobel. Then we decide if we rescue her and how we leave New York City. And where we actually go from here.'

'Thatsoundsstraightforward,Chase.'

'Why are you talking like that, Geepy?' Chase peers at me.

'Because,' I add, 'if I say things really fast, then I won't realise how stressed I am.'

Chase smiles. '*Relax*. Really. Because compared to the stress that's going to kick in later today, this is nothing!'

I would give Chase a dirty look, but the pancakes and coffees have arrived, and I can't see over or around them.

'If I turn into a caffeine addict, Chase . . .' I'm not sure how much Chase can hear, as I'm speaking directly into a stack of sound-absorbent pancakes. '*You* can pay for the re-hab. Our family is in *total* agreement that a brisk walk, a crisp apple, or a cold cotton face washer is far more beneficial health-wise than anything that arrives in a cup.'

There. That should keep him quiet!

We leave the diner and hit the street. I feel rather full and a bit jumpy. Correction: I feel really, *really* full and extremely jumpy.

'Don't look now,' Chase whispers. 'But there's a dude in sunglasses and a black overcoat trailing us.'

I swing around so fast that I feel dizzy. 'Who!? Where!? What!? Let's go! Hit the wire, men! Roll!

Jump! Run! Hide!' Boy, I don't even know *where* this stuff is coming from. 'Fire teams Alpha and Delta, go, go, go!'

Chase pushes me up hard against a brick wall.

'Calm *down*,' he hisses. 'Be cool. Just do what I do, and everything will be fine. Now *run!*'

I take off after Chase, dodging around people like a pancake-filled pinball. He cuts across the road, horns blasting at him, then we sprint down an alley, past dumpsters (I cover my mouth) and along another narrow street between tall buildings criss-crossed with rusty fire escapes.

'In that blue doorway and up the stairs, George!'

This is more PE than I've done in my whole life. But as I'm currently a caffeine-fuelled pancake-powered crazy man, I pound up the steps, my knees going like pistons. Then I follow Chase into a shop selling the strangest underwear I've ever seen.

Correction: I've *never* seen it, but it looks to lack support where you'd need it most. And in my candid opinion, it would be a nightmare to wash and fold.

'In there!' Chase points to a sign saying, *Vintage World*. 'Quick.'

We've plunged into a place that smells like my Great Grandma Edith's lounge room, which doubled as an indoor exercise space for her prize-winning ferrets and a drying room for recycled wheat bags. There are racks and racks of old clothes everywhere.

'Grab an outfit, George!' Chase whacks a yellow cap on his head. 'And put it on!'

I snatch a rather nice outfit in dark brown then dash behind a red velvet curtain. Chase is in the cubicle next door.

'Ready, George?'

'Almost,' I say, doing up the buttons of my woody-coloured knee breeches. 'I'm all set for a round of golf in 1910!' From head to toe, I am a picture of old-fashioned, brown, golfing elegance.

'Get out here, then!'

I shove my own clothes in a bag and step out. Chase is now a jockey wearing shiny black boots, white silk pants, a green shirt, and a yellow cap.

'Tally ho, old chap,' he says, 'let's—'

From behind another curtain appears a tall thin man. He's dressed as an old-style ship's captain, possibly from the *Titanic*, because he looks as if fish have been nibbling at him for the last one hundred years.

'Hello, darling boys!' He rests one pale spidery hand on his chin. 'Would you like to stay for tea?

Or just give me—' he growls like a maniac, '—one hundred bucks right *now*.'

Chase pulls out his leather jacket from my bag.

'This is worth a thousand dollars,' he says. 'Throw in a couple of those sailor suits and call it a deal.'

The captain's blue eyes glint like cut glass. 'Done!' Somehow the jacket disappears and we are holding two white sailor suits, complete with round caps and silver whistles. 'See ya soon, boys.'

'Not if we see you first.' Chase taps his cap with his whip. 'Ta-ta, Captain Creepy.'

'Toodle-ooh,' I add, which I would never say if I hadn't drunk two litres of black coffee with seven sugars. 'Goodbye to you.'

Then we go down the steps and sneak out onto the street. In my dark-brown golfing outfit, I feel nicely disguised, although people seem to be staring at us. Chase laughs, swinging along, smacking his whip against his boot. Suddenly, the guy who was chasing us is directly in front of us.

'Excuse me, ah, young gentlemen.' His sunglasses reflect our faces. 'Have you seen two boys about your height around here? They're Australians. And they're lost. Their mothers are worried sick.'

I see a black gun in a black holster under the guy's arm. Pulse rate one-ninety and climbing!

'We ain't seen no Orstralians,' Chase says. 'But if we do, sir, whot? Give 'em a meat pie or somefink?'

The man reaches into his coat — pulse rate two hundred! — and hands Chase a white card.

'There's a reward,' the man says. 'Five hundred thousand dollars. Call this number.'

'I will, good sir.' Chase takes the card. 'You can count on me.'

The man is gone. We shakily walk on. Chase dumps the card.

'If they catch us,' he says, 'they'll hold us to ransom for two hundred and fifty million dollars. Which my dad can't pay. Then *bang*! We're off to the big country club in the sky.'

Gulp!

'But!' Chase drags me up the street. 'Perhaps we can get enough money to give my dad a chance to make back what he lost.'

Or lose some more!

We make it back to the apartment and rest on the couch. To take my mind off the kidnap threat, I think about my home-grown algae project, which is going alarmingly well, according to an email sent by our next-door neighbour, Bob Bobbington. He says that it has taken over the entire backyard.

'Any shares you fancy on Wall Street?' Chase asks. 'Anything that'll go up by ten thousand per cent in twenty-four hours or less?'

'None,' I answer. 'Besides, we haven't got any money anyway, have we? That fifty million's been frozen.'

Chase nods. 'But we have to keep thinking, Georgie. Come on, kid. Hit me with *something*!'

I take a deep breath. 'Well, my home-grown algae project needs investment, Chase. If my dad's theory's right, algae can power every car on the planet. And our algae, the Parker Super Algae 2000, we estimate, can grow one hundred times faster than all other algae ever seen.'

Chase shifts a silk cushion. 'How much money do you need?'

That's a very good question. 'I did hear my dad say seven hundred and fifty, Chase. Which is a lot, I know. But we're in a race with the Russians, although theirs is frozen over for winter.'

Chase nods. 'Seven hundred and fifty thousand? Or seven hundred and fifty *million*?'

I'm in shock. 'No, Chase. Seven hundred and fifty *dollars*. For a new plastic pond, a longer hose, and a scoop net.'

Chase claps once. 'When we get cash, we'll do it, definitely.'

Wow! When people *even* look at our algae, they generally just hold their noses and slowly back out the side gate.

'We'll go to the hospital after lunch,' Chase says. 'And we'll go in these outfits. Best to keep the kidnappers guessing.' He stretches. 'Otherwise they might grab Isobel instead of us. Now, some pizza, because we've got big things ahead of us.'

CHAPTER FIFTEEN

We have a hot and spicy chilli Mexican pizza that seems to have taken over where my caffeine levels left off.

'Tabasco sauce, George?' Chase holds out a little red bottle. 'Watch out. It's hot.'

'Sure!' I splash it on, take a bite, then almost hit the roof. 'Whoo-eey, that *is* hot! Damn hot!' I get up and do a little dance. 'That is truly *smokin'*! Yeah, mama, *that's* what I'm talkin' about! Kaboom *shaboom feel the temperature in the room!*'

Chase looks a little puzzled. '*What?*'

'I dunno, bro!' I spin seven hundred and twenty degrees. 'Ah'm just high on red chilli with a green chilli chaser, Chase! I'm a ragin' rattlesnake rarin' to go!'

'Calm down, Parkie.' Chase pours me a large glass of milk. 'We're going to have to make some very serious life and death decisions.'

I slide across the room and take the glass right out of Chase's hand.

'No problem!' I drink it in one hit. 'Calcium, Chase! I got bones of steel and fists of iron! I'll pole-vault the pain barrier, swim with sharks, and *wrassle* me an alligator!'

Chase guides me to the couch. 'Save your energy and keep quiet. We have to be prepared.'

I listen hard. 'Oh, I'm ready, Chaser-roony! I'm a flashing light and a screaming siren. I'm a—'

Chase pokes me. 'Enough, George! Enough!'

Leaving the apartment, we meet Clemmy at the lift.

'The advertising people wouldn't advance me any money,' she says. 'But I've got a ten-year supply of toothpaste. Here, have some.'

'Don't mind if I do!' I take three tubes. 'Yo, baby, I'm Filling-Free George! I'm the boss with the floss! And don't forget those big babies up the back! That's tough territory there in molar land!'

Clemmy looks at Chase. 'What's up with him?'

Chase grips my arm. 'A little too much of every-thing. He'll be right in a few minutes.'

'I'm right *right now*,' I yell. 'I'm—'

Chase clamps a hand over my mouth and pushes me into the lift.

To save money, Chase and I walk fifteen blocks to the John J Hospital hospital. As we look up at the big building, I estimate my pulse is down around ninety beats per minute. Nervousness has replaced my chilli-pizza-fuelled adrenaline rush.

'My parents fly in to visit Isobel,' Chase says. 'But she's always the same. So they don't come very often. They're busy. You know how it is.'

I do know what it's like to not see your parents very often. But if I was sick, I'm sure my mother and father wouldn't leave me stranded in another country.

'Well,' I say, '*we're* here, Chase.' We sit on a seat on the hospital lawn. 'What's our plan of attack? If Isobel leaves, won't there be bills to be paid? And how will we get to Australia when we can't buy jet fuel or buy air tickets? We can't even get to the airport!'

Chase clicks his tongue thoughtfully. 'We'll see Izzy, then consider our options.'

'Anyway, she'll be pleased to see you, Chase,' I add. 'No matter what happens.'

He nods. 'But imagine if we have to leave her here?'

'Whatever we decide,' I add, 'will be for the best. So let's go.'

CHAPTER SIXTEEN

We ask the patient-information officer where we might find Isobel Landon-Bond. Large security guards in black jackets and white shirts keep a close eye on us. The information officer, a woman dressed in a frilly pink shirt, looks at us through blue-mirrored glasses.

'Only members of the Landon-Bond family are allowed to visit Isobel,' she says. 'Are you two, er, related, whatever?'

'Certainly,' says Chase, in a posh English accent. 'We are Isobel's first cousins from the Lake District in Upper-Lower Buckinghamshire-on-Padleigh Pond via Crickleton Wood. And you American folk have been very welcoming and lovely.' Chase looks at me. 'Haven't they, Dicky?'

'Absolutely, Alfie,' I confirm. 'The quintessential bees-knees.'

The lady puts her finger on a bright red button marked 'Security'.

'Young Dicky is a gifted poet and collector of antique cricket bats and wooden buckets,' Chase says. 'His English is of an old-fashioned type best used at flower and vegetable shows.'

The woman studies me. 'I guess he really *is* English then. Fifteenth floor,' she says. 'A nurse will let you in. Have a *nice* day.' She glares at me.

We hustle away and take the lift to the fifteenth floor. Chase looks stressed.

'You can only cross one bridge at a time, Chase,' I say. 'Trying to cross more than one implies a human being can split into multiple entities, and well, ha, that's just a silly and confusing concept.' Right, I think I've cleared things up to a point where we both feel quite a bit brighter!

A small female nurse taps a door code – which I memorise – into a keypad.

'Isobel is a beautiful young lady,' the nurse says smiling sadly. 'She is a gifted artist and makes divine jewellery. But she is silent. She does not like loud noises or sudden movements.'

We enter the room, the door locking swiftly

behind us. Sitting at the window is a slim, pale girl with long dark hair and dreamy blue eyes.

'Isobel,' Chase says. 'It's me, Chase. And my friend, George.'

Isobel stands and slowly a smile appears on her face.

'Hello, Isobel.' I see some amazing paintings – portraits of Isobel – on the wall, signed by her. 'I go to school with Chase.'

She nods gently.

'I missed you, Isobel.' Chase walks across the room and hugs her. 'Are you okay? You look well.'

Isobel picks up a pad and pencil from a small table.

I miss everyone, she writes. *I am lonely. I want to go home.*

Chase paces around the room, saying nothing. Then he stops pacing, as if he has come to a decision.

'We'll take you home.' He nods. 'Tomorrow. Georgie-boy and I'll work it out. But don't tell *anyone*. Not a single soul.'

Isobel studies Chase. I see she has a long silver scar across her forehead. Again she writes on the pad.

Thank you. I love you both. I know you will help me.

Without warning, a tall lady in a white coat – a doctor, presumably – enters the room. I suppose she could be a pastry cook, although, let's face it, that would be unusual in this situation.

'I'm Doctor Theodora Welk. I oversee Isobel's treatment. I believe you are relatives from ye olde merry England or whatever you call it these days.'

Chase advances, smiling. 'Dear Doctor,' he says, 'I am Lord Alfred Landon-Bond the Third, and this is my terribly wealthy brother, Sir Dicky. But don't let's get caught up with that old royal family rubbish, eh?'

'Oh, don't worry, I won't.' Doctor Welk sniffs. 'Due to Isobel's head injury, she cannot fly on an aeroplane. She will stay with us for another year. At least. By then, she may speak. She's a fascinating case. Quite odd.'

Isobel is crying silently. Referring to someone as odd when they are in the room is extremely rude. I have experienced it myself, once at the hands of a shopping-centre Santa, whose ideas about the North Pole and worldwide parcel delivery were far more odd than I've ever been.

'You're the doctor, Doctor Welk,' says Chase.

'I am,' she says. 'Now I'm off to have afternoon coffee with my friends in the mortuary. Perhaps I'll see you in a year? Maybe two.'

Chase nods. 'We'll advise her Australian family of what you've told us. It's been *most* informative.'

'You do that.' Doctor Welk produces a smile as thin as a wire. 'Because her parents are somewhat hard to catch up with. And take a few of Isobel's paintings with you. We throw them out at the end of each week.' Then she leaves, thank goodness.

Suddenly, and with difficulty, Isobel speaks.

'She . . . is . . . a . . .'

We wait. Perspiration has appeared on Isobel's forehead.

'. . . *witch.*'

I couldn't agree more.

Chase and I leave the hospital, storing as many details about fire escapes, exits, entrances, lifts, security guards, and stairs as we can.

'I don't mean to be a party pooper, Chase,' I say, as we walk back to Fourth Avenue. 'But if we get Isobel out, then what? We can't take her on the jet because of her injury. And we don't have any money to go home any other way.'

Chase leapfrogs a fire hydrant. 'Since we can't fly,' he explains, 'Clemmy's going to sell the plane. And Mr X has sold the jacket factory and done a deal with Rhibeeyonceyh. We've got money, George, in theory,' Chase picks up a coin off the pavement, 'but in reality, we've barely got a dime. Hopefully Mr X will sort that out tonight.'

'How?' I say, as Franz, the top-hatted doorman at our apartment block, lets us in. 'Thank you, Franz,' I add. 'We'll give you a tip when we get our . . . spending money.'

Chase's phone rings. He answers, nods, then ends the call.

'We meet Mr X's guy tonight at ten. By the Hudson River. Oh, and FYI, he's a dog.'

I'm a little confused by Chase's last statement. 'Um, Chase,' I say, 'just for your information, I don't know what FYI stands for. So, for my information, could you please explain it?'

Chase stares at me. 'That's what it stands for, George. For Your Information.'

'Oh, really? How clever,' I answer. 'Well, FYI, I've never heard of that before. Anyway, what sort of dog will we be looking for?'

Chase shrugs. 'One with plenty of cash, I hope.'

There's nothing I can say to that.

CHAPTER SEVENTEEN

Clemmy, surrounded by colourful shopping bags, is watching television.

'I sold the jet,' she tells us. 'And bought a few things. I'll be off to LA tomorrow for some TV work. I'm sure we'll catch up in one country or another. How's Isobel?'

Chase and I collapse onto the couch.

'Kind of okay,' Chase says. 'The hospital wants to keep her for another year. But we're going to take her home.'

'Good on you.' Clemmy nods. 'How will you get her there?'

'Ship.' Chase sits up. 'You don't get sea-sick, do you, George?'

I've never been on a ship. Or a bicycle, skateboard, or roller skates. I did try an eight-wheel safety scooter once, but it seemed to be possessed by the devil.

'I don't know, Chase,' I say. 'And anyway, how will we find a ship going to where we want to go?'

'We'll work that out,' Chase says. 'After we've met the dog with the dollars at the Williamsburg Bridge.'

'We should take Amy,' I suggest. 'Dogs can communicate with other dogs, as you would expect. I think she'd be a big help.'

Chase and I dress in our darkest clothes, pack Amy in one of Clemmy's shopping bags, then head out into the cold, siren-filled New York night. Franz hails us a cab and we set off for the Williamsburg Bridge.

'You ain't them dopey Aussie bad-boys on TV, are you?' The blonde driver studies us as she zooms along. 'Them ones who owe like a billion bucks? Because nasty people is after them for the big *reward*.'

Oh, dear!

'Ve're not dopey Oz-tralians,' Chase says. 'Ve're smart *Austrians*. Aren't ve, George?'

'Oh, *ja*,' I say. 'Ve are Austrians from ze Vienna Boys Choir who sing Gott Bless America every zingle day. And you chapz won ze war fair and zquare. No worriez about zat.'

The lady stops the taxi under a bridge by the river and Chase pays her our last few dollars.

'Take care now,' she says, although I'm not sure she means it.

'*Danke*, dear.' Chase shuts the door. 'Let's find this dog and get out of here. I'm not sure that old bat bought the Austrian thing. What time is it?'

I hit the button on my watch. 'Five to ten.' It occurs to me this is the latest I've ever stayed up in my whole life. Wow!

Chase points. 'There's the bridge. Stay low, and let's hope it's dog-friendly.'

I'm more concerned whether we're about to meet a friendly *dog*, but I keep quiet.

We climb up onto the long, dark bridge, and let Amy out of the bag.

'How will the money-dog know the time, Chase?' I ask.

'Don't ask me.' Chase shrugs. 'Even though you just did.'

I see Amy tilt her head to one side and look expectantly up the river. Suddenly a helicopter with a blindingly bright white searchlight sweeps towards us on a hurricane of sound.

'Behind the pylon, Chase!' I grab Amy. 'Get down!'

We huddle as the helicopter hovers. The noise is incredible and the light beam turns everything silver. Then, thankfully, the chopper moves away, and I see a large dog running towards us, like a lone wolf on a Siberian plain. It's a German shepherd, which is a breed I would normally change suburbs to avoid, but not this time. We call out.

'Here, doggy! C'mon, feller! Good boy!'

Amy lets go five sharp barks and the big dog runs in right on top of us, wagging its tail and licking our faces. I see it wears a harness with a small backpack.

'Pat him, George!' Chase is stuffing bundles of money into Clemmy's pink shopping bag. 'Right. I've got the dough. Let him go and let's split!'

I try to send the dog back across the bridge but it's more interested in playing with Amy.

'Go, big feller!' I say. 'Home!' I turn to Chase. 'You don't have a stick, do you, because dogs—'

'Oh, yeah,' Chase says. 'I've got a whole bundle.' Then he shouts. 'Of course I don't have a stick!'

The German shepherd looks downstream, cries once then takes off like a golden streak. Now I see why.

'The chopper's coming back!' I yell. 'Run!' And as

I'm about to, I accidentally step on the shopping bag and rip a hole in it. Out falls the money.

'Grab the dough, George!' Chase grabs four big bundles. 'Quick!'

I pick up three more, Amy grabs the last by its rubber band, and we sprint towards the road.

'Go, GP!' Chase pushes me. 'Faster, faster. It's coming!'

The chopper roars in, lighting up the bridge like a tinsel Christmas tree, the three of us running for our lives. With a sinking feeling, I see Amy's teeth have broken the rubber band around the fat bundle of money, leaving a trail of green notes whirling away like leaves. *Oh, that's not so good*, I think. But I keep on running and Chase keeps on yelling.

'Down the steps, Georgie! Go!'

We make it safely under the bridge and gradually, thankfully, the sound of the helicopter dies away. As we catch our breath I see what appear to be butterflies fluttering into the river. I look down and Amy looks up, wagging her tail, holding one wet hundred-dollar bill.

'Good dog,' I say, adding the soggy note to my bundle, and hoping Chase doesn't notice.

'What d'you mean, *good* dog?' Chase *has* noticed. 'She just lost us fifty thousand freakin' dollars!'

I can see that's not great news. 'Um, it's only money,' I say. 'That's what my dear old dad says.'

'That's because he hasn't got any damn money.' Chase holds up a hand and a yellow taxi stops. 'Let's just go,' he says tiredly. 'It's too dangerous to try and get any of it back now. Come on.'

Another of my dad's sayings is, *Easy come, easy go*, but I think I'll just keep that to myself at this point.

CHAPTER EIGHTEEN

We catch a taxi back to Fourth Avenue, stopping once to buy some fruit, as my toilet habits require a certain amount of fibre to stay on schedule, especially with all the stress of the last few days.

'This ship, Chase,' I say. 'How will we find one?'

The taxi driver, a small black-eyed man wearing a red bandana and gold earrings, coughs.

'Er-hergm, dudes! You cats want to catch a ship? Where you cats want to go?'

If I say Australia, he might put two and two together and come up with a big fat reward.

'Oh, France,' I say, since Chase did mention it. 'Paris is lovely. Not as lovely as New York, of course. But you know, *nice*. Ish.'

The driver nods. 'I kin git you on a cruise ship leaving tomorrow night. Because my bro, Harley, knows a guy who knows a guy who knows a dude.'

'Right on!' Chase snaps his fingers. 'You gotta number?'

'If you got cash,' the driver says. 'I most certainly definitely positively have.'

So, it seems we're part of the way out of the USA!

CHAPTER NINETEEN

Chase and I say goodbye to Clemmy down on Fourth Avenue. Somehow she's managed to hitch a lift to Los Angeles in a US Air Force Blackbird spy plane flying via Cuba.

'Be careful, boys!' She waves from the taxi. 'I'd send you an aerial photograph of Havana, but then I'd have to kill you! Say hi to Isobel.'

We watch as the taxi bullies its way out into the traffic. It concerns me where exactly Clemmy's going to put her suitcase on a Blackbird spy plane.

'On a number of occasions, Chase,' I say, 'to fill in a quiet weekend, I've looked at the online cross-sectional blueprints of the Blackbird. No luggage rack or glove box that I could see.'

'Oh, they'll whack it in somewhere.' Chase seems sure about this. 'You know, it's like going on holidays. Everything just fits in the end. Now let's go up to the roof garden and work out how we're going to rescue Isobel.'

From twenty stories up, the city of New York looks like it would weigh down the earth with its hundreds of skyscrapers.

'What's our plan, Chase?' I watch Amy playing with a baseball we found. 'Isobel's room is extremely high security.'

'We keep it simple.' Chase talks slowly. 'We walk in. We walk out with Isobel. If we sneak around, people will get suspicious.'

'Yes, but if we don't sneak around,' I say, 'we'll get caught. The staff watched us like hawks.'

Chase nods. 'But would they notice two boy scouts doing their good deed for the day? I think not. So we'll adapt our school shirts and carry some flowers or something. Two scouts go in. Three go out. Easy.'

I'm confused. 'Where do we get the third boy scout from, Chase?'

Chase crosses his eyes. 'It'll be *Isobel*, George. My *sister*. Are you *with* me?'

'Oh yes, I am now,' I say. 'I was somewhat confused because, historically, scouts are always boys and clearly Isobel's—'

Chase holds up a finger. 'Your next job, with your amazing memory, is to accurately construct our scout uniforms, okay?'

'Absolutely no problem with the shirts,' I say. 'Or the scarves, sock tabs, or merit badges. But the woggle will be tricky, Chase. And if we're just pretending to do good deeds, that's against international scout law. Meaning, if we're caught telling lies, that'd be the end of our scouting days, Chase, forever.'

'I can live with that.' Chase pokes me. 'Just get a wriggle on and get those woggles made!'

We stand, just as I see Amy drop the baseball, which rolls down a gutter, speeds up, then flies over the edge. Uh-oh.

'Hmm,' says Chase. 'I think we'd better disappear.'

We quickly turn our school shirts into uniforms of the Ninth Tapley New York Scout Troop. I then convert a floral tea towel into scarves and glue merit badges on our shirts for everything from Safe Mousetrap Setting to Removing Racoons from Chimneys.

'Where are the woggles for the scarves?' Chase asks, as we drink tea (Tea-Making is another merit badge I have).

I show Chase. The woggles are braided from white drinking straws. From a distance, they look great, but close up they look more like cold spaghetti.

'We'll need something for our good deed,' Chase says. 'Perhaps we should take some of those flowers or some fruit from the kitchen? What about that box of cigars in the lounge?'

The flowers have wilted, the bananas are soft, and cigars would be a dead giveaway because I would think the International Scouting Movement is a non-smoking organisation, with the obvious exception of campfires (as long as they were lit under the supervision of a person with a Campfire Safety merit badge, a Level One or Two Certificate in Fire Extinguisher Handling, and reasonable eyesight).

'Give me thirty minutes,' I say. 'I've got an idea. Or two, actually.'

I've quickly made up a pair of rather entertaining little booklets. One I've filled with hilarious GPNPGRJs (George Parker No Parental Guidance Required Jokes). The other contains a selection of toe-tapping bush tunes and catchy sea songs from yesteryear that appeal to people of all ages who appreciate skill-based lyrics coupled with rhythms that even the non-musical can enjoy.

'Which do you want, Chase?' I hold up the booklets. 'The George Parker Very Hilarious Joke Book? Or the George Parker Cheerful Sing-Along Songster Companion? Both will undoubtedly prove useful, educational, and entertaining.'

Chase seems amused, although he hasn't looked at either book.

'Give me an example,' he says, 'of a hilarious George Parker joke.'

Easy. All my jokes are pressure-tested on my chums down at the Tapley Chess Club, and it's no exaggeration to say that if you can get a chuckle from the chaps at the Chargers, then normal people will probably be two, three, or four times as amused. So, here goes with a George Parker Hilarious Joke.

I clear my throat. Oh boy, this one's an absolute killer!

'Chase, what do you call a boomerang that won't come back?'

'A stick,' says Chase.

'Well, it could be that, I suppose,' I say. 'But *my* punch line is an aerodynamic boo-boo made with an inappropriately shaped projectile resulting in an

annoying aeronautical afternoon for all concerned.'
I can't help but laugh even if it *is* my own joke, with
side-splitting George Parker aero-spatial engineering
modifications to keep it fresh. 'See? Hilarious.'

Chase is laughing so much he's crying.

'Oh, yes, hilarious, Georgie-boy.' Chase holds his
ribs. 'You might possibly be the best kid in the world.'

That's doubtful.

Chase wipes his eyes and takes a steadying
breath.

'Okay. We go in five. I estimate we'll be back in
three hours, ready to leave the country with Isobel.
Take this.' Chase hands me a wad of money. 'We
might have to buy our way out.'

'Why wouldn't they just let us out of the hospital
the way we came in?' I ask. 'We're scouts performing
a social service, not criminals breaking the law.'

'I wouldn't bet on it.' Chase tightens his woggle.
'We have to *be prepared* for any *emergency*. That's a
scout thing.'

Speaking of emergencies, I think as I take the
money, I wouldn't mind purchasing a packet of peppermints, as peppermint naturally soothes the inner
workings of a person's bowels. This is a fun medical fact
not widely enough known or appreciated, especially

by those who suffer from, let's say, certain *challenges* downstairs.

'Right, Georgie-boy.' Chase gives me a three-fingered salute. 'Let's hit the road to freedom and France!'

CHAPTER TWENTY

We successfully bypass the John J Hospital hospital information desk and step into an empty lift.

'How many patients will we cheer up before we free Isobel?' I ask Chase. 'Some of the old songs about pulling up sails and boiling whale blubber are quite tiring to act out.'

'Are you joking, George?' Chase looks at me seriously.

'Not at all.' I shake my head. 'A patient would hardly be helped if a singing scout collapsed after one song of the sea too many. It might tip them over the edge.'

Chase holds up the joke book. 'These things are *props*. They're part of our *disguise*. We're not going to *use* them. We're here to get Isobel out and that's that.'

Oh, I see how this works, and it's somewhat disappointing.

'It's a shame,' I say, 'that we don't get to share a salty

sea shanty or a wonderful joke with these poor folk before they walk through death's door, Chase. But you're the boss.'

The lift stops and a large lady dressed in a yellow bird suit shuffles in.

'You're late.' Her beady black eyes bore into us over a pointy yellow beak. 'I thought being on time was a scout thing. Anyway, I have a room of sick patients waiting. So don't give me any crap. Get goin', you two.' She pokes us out of the lift with yellow flowers made of wire. 'Or I'll report you to Troop Leader Roger. And as you know, he was in the Mafia for twenty years, so he's not a person you want to annoy.'

Through an open door, I see a room full of people. Some are in wheelchairs, some have bandages around their heads, and many are attached to oxygen bottles. And they look grumpy, which is understandable, if they don't have long to live. Yes, it looks like I have no choice but to get this show on the road!

'Joke or song?' I whisper to Chase. 'To start the fun.'

'Hit 'em with your best shot.' Chase backs away. 'I'll wait in the wings.'

I make my entrance, going straight into a George Parker extended dance-mix of 'Old Man Emu'. And might I say, I accurately impersonate every Australian native bird and animal while carrying the tune right to the end. And the crowd like it a lot! I turn to Chase but he's gone, leaving my George Parker joke book on a seat.

Okay folks, get ready to laugh, no matter how lousy you feel!

I open my joke book and see I've cracked it for a beauty. This one had the Chargers in stitches for eleven minutes!

'What happens when it's raining cats and dogs?' I scan the happy faces. Nobody has any idea, as I expected. 'Well, according to the Bureau of Meteorology, it's impossible,' I say, to add suspense, 'but if it did rain cats and dogs, guess what?' I wait, as one thing I am good at is comic timing. 'You might step in a *poodle*!'

Yes! Not a puddle but a POODLE!

And the crowd goes wild!

So it's back to the song book, from where I pick out 'Kookaburra Sits in the Old Gumtree' to sing in rounds. This I do by dividing the room up into People Who've Had An Organ Transplant, People Whose Operation Didn't Go So Well, and Those Who Might Not See Next Week.

Now *that's* what I call sensitive song-selection *and* good scouting!

Approximately fifteen minutes later, I'm just about out of material. The crowd has also gone a little flat after one lady was taken to the Intensive Care Unit during the 'Banana Boat' song. Sadly, she was pronounced Dead on Arrival, but I'm pleased to tell the survivors that she did have her Organ Donor card all filled in and ready to go, so we're soon back on track and feeling fine.

'And on that bright note,' I add, 'here's a cheery ballad called, "A Strapping Young Stockman Lay Dying". What he's dying of, I'm not sure. Perhaps he fell off his horse or got bitten by a snake, who knows? But if anyone's interested in the answer, perhaps we can google it later.'

'Pssst!' Chase is at the door. 'Wind it up, George! Code Red!'

I see another scout with Chase, which is quite the coincidence. Then I realise that it's Isobel!

'Gotta go, kids!' I kangaroo-hop backwards to the door. 'I love you all and keep on breathing, if you can!' Then we're in the lift and heading down, down, down.

A faint smile takes over Isobel's face.

'Hi, George,' she whispers.

'Hi, Isobel.' I see she looks worried, as if she has gone through a lot of difficulties for a long time. 'It's a sunny day outside,' I add. 'Really quite beautiful.'

The lift stops and a little old lady in a bright green dress and purple hair steps in. She's holding a collection tin.

'Hello, girls.' She peers at us from under a red tennis visor. 'Some nasty Austrian air-force boys have kidnapped a patient from the fifteenth floor. The place is in lockdown. There's no way out. *No* way.'

It seems quite unusual that the Luftwaffe would be involved in something like this – and then I realise she's talking about us!

'If we see them,' I say, 'I'll dial 9-1-1 and Homeland Security. Now, what charity are you collecting for, madam?' I take out the money Chase gave me.

'I'm collecting for Sydney the Patient Companion Dog.' She pushes the tin into my chest. 'Is that a ten or a twenty, dear?'

I add another ten. 'It's twenty now.' I poke the money into the slot. 'Where does Sydney the Companion Dog live?'

'At home,' says the old lady. 'But he's also got a pen in the serenity garden on the ground floor. With a doggy-door that opens right out into the street.' She holds the tin higher. 'You can meet Sydney, if you like. And see his doggy-door.'

I flick off notes, poke them in the tin, and keep on poking until we crawl out the doggy-door and catch the first cab we see back to our apartment. I do feel guilty about bribing our way out of the hospital, but seeing Sydney the Companion Dog tucking into a steak and caviar sandwich, I know it's all for a good cause.

We eat lunch, Isobel has a sleep, and Chase rings the taxi guy who knows the ship dude.

'Have you heard anything from your parents, Chase?' I ask. 'About the, er, lost money?'

Chase sighs. 'Yeah, Dad's paid back two million. But they're being quite stubborn about the other two hundred and forty eight. And they've frozen the money Clemmy got for the plane. So my folks thought it safest to hide out in the Italian Riviera in a small castle on a six-star island.'

I'm not sure that's a place I would've picked, but I suppose it would be more comfortable than, say, a tent in a caravan park in southern Tasmania.

'So these people,' I say hesitantly, 'would still like to get hold of us?'

'Oh, you bet,' says Chase. 'And the hospital sent Dad a bill for three million bucks. I mean, he'll pay it. Just not yet. Since he hasn't got the money.'

Yes, that normally would hold up proceedings. Chase's phone rings.

'Okay,' he answers. 'Good. Fine. Right. No problem. Sure. Excellent. Great. Terrific.'

That sounds reasonably positive.

'Near the kiosk?' Chase talks very clearly. 'At five bells? Of the Last Dog Watch? Right.' He ends the call and looks at me. 'What the hell does all *that* rubbish mean?'

Fortunately for us, I use the official maritime bell system for my bath-time tugboat and container ship activities, so this is easily cleared up.

'Five bells of the Last Dog Watch is six thirty p.m.,' I say. 'Obviously.'

Chase grins. 'You're a genius, George. Right. Sailor suits on and let's go!'

'Those suits are a hundred years old, Chase,' I say. 'We'll look ridiculous.'

'No, it's cool.' He drums his fists on my knees. 'The ship dude, Roland, is in charge of Onboard Entertainment. We're now *actors*, George. People will *expect* us to look odd.'

'What about Isobel, Chase?' I'm worried. 'We can't expect her to present a ten-minute version of *Romeo and Juliet* on the docks. Or get her head around my many hilarious jokes or favourite folk songs. Can she play the gumleaf or the spoons?'

'Nah.' Chase heads to the fridge. 'She can just sit on a suitcase and be a prop. *Improvisation*, George. That's the name of the *acting* game! Want an apple?'

I'd better, because my bowels are telling me quite clearly that I'm stressed. Just to be on the safe side, I pop a couple of peppermints that I picked up with the fruit. Then we pack, grab Isobel and Amy, and head for lift. Franz the doorman, wearing his white gloves, is very pleased to see us.

'Oh, hullo liddle zailor boy!' He pinches my cheek. 'Everybotty loves a zailor!'

'We're actually actors *acting* as sailors,' I explain to Franz. 'We're also mime artists. You've heard of Marcel Marceau?' I correct myself. 'Well, you won't actually have *heard him*, Franz, as mimes don't speak unless they've struck a problem. Or are buying, for example, a railway ticket or a pair of trousers, and so forth.'

Franz looks fascinated. 'Oh, *ja-ja*,' he says. 'Marcel wore white gluffs. Like zeze.' He pulls a spare pair from his pocket and gives them to me. 'Zee you zailor boyz! Gut luck under ze bright lightz.'

I tip Franz twenty dollars as we get into the cab. Then we set off to the wharf and hopefully, eventually, to France.

CHAPTER
TWENTY-ONE

At five bells on the dot, we arrive at the old timber kiosk on the wharf. Our ship is moored further down the dock. She has a black hull, white upper decks, and is called the *Titania*, which reminds me of something but I can't think what.

'How will we identify Roland?' I ask Chase, as I finish my Junior Jumbo coffee and let Amy out of my backpack.

'He'll be wearing a red beret and carrying a cane.' Chase looks around. 'When he sees us, he'll do a five-second tap-dance, then you'll do the same.'

'Me?' I stare at Chase. 'Why don't you?'

'Because you need the practice.' Chase smiles. 'Anyway, break a leg! As they say in Hollywood.'

Who says that? Someone who has no feelings, that's who!

I see a thin fellow dressed in black walk onto the wharf. He holds a cane, wears a red beret, and has a pointy black moustache. Suddenly he does a hop, skip, step, jump then turns on his heels to point at the ship with his stick. Chase elbows me.

'That's Roland, George! Dance, Parkie, dance!'

I wait for the caffeine to help me along, but it doesn't seem to be having any effect.

'Go, George!' Chase hisses. 'Do it in memory of Michael Jackson!'

'Michael *who*?'

Chase pushes me, but unfortunately Amy has hold of my shoelace. I trip, grab a pole and swing right around it. Then I stop to tuck my shirt and singlet in, only to see Amy heading for a road pounding with traffic. I flash forward, scoop her up, dodge a taxi and find myself hard up against the door of a public toilet – which opens, and in I go!

'Whoops! Pardon, madam!'

And out I come, managing to shut the door behind me as I juggle Amy, who decides she'd prefer to be with Isobel. So I put the dog down, which people mistake for me bowing, and so they start to clap and throw money into my sailor cap, which had fallen off at the beginning of this entire dancing disaster. So there's only one thing to say, I suppose, and that's:

'Thank you and *goodnight*!'

Roland heads for a small crew-only gangplank, pushing rudely through the crowd of waiting passengers and officials.

'Excuze *moi*, peazants!' He waves his cane. 'Get out of ze way! Zeze actors 'ave talent you can only dream about! Zey can pretend to be treez or even an 'opping animal like a konckaroo or an upzet perzon who haz lozt zere tail-wigging pippy dock in ze off-ze-lead dock park!'

We follow him up the gangplank, everything going smoothly until three large customs officers stop us and ask Roland some rather pointed questions.

'Who are these people?'

Roland tells the largest officer that we're actors.

Next question. 'Where are they going?'

'Beaudiful France,' Roland informs the second medium-sized officer.

The third officer, quite short with a thick black moustache, snorts.

'So how do we really *know* they're actors, buddy?'

Boom, the caffeine kicks in! Mentally, I replay every mime act I've ever seen, which is pretty much always about a person stuck on the wrong side of a glass door, or a person walking into a strong wind. Then, deciding to combine the two, I get into silent action!

'Oh, *look*,' says Roland, patting me on the head. 'Poor Gheorge iz ztuck on ze wrong zide of ze glaz door and ze ztronk wind iz makink iz face zo fonny. What can 'ee do?'

I push through the non-existent gale-force wind, then pretend to feel around the invisible door. Then I pretend to walk straight into the invisible door. Next, I stand hands-on-hips and look totally confused by this invisible door that's proving to be such an obstacle, and then I do a kind of windmilling action like a tree in a storm, as the non-existent wind is very powerful. Then, when I'm running out of options, one of the officers laughs, steps forward, and pretends to open the invisible door from the inside!

Voilà!

So I simply let the non-existent wind blow me through the now-open invisible door, bow graciously, and signal for my actor friends to follow with our luggage. And in two minutes, we are in our cabin and much relieved.

'*Gheorge*,' Roland says, 'you will be in my zuperbly

brilliant acting show, for sure.' Then he turns to Chase. 'Now give me two zousand Yankee dollars, Chaze, or you will all be in jail until you are died.'

Chase hands over a stack of bills, which Roland tucks under his beret.

'*Merci*.' Roland turns to me. 'I have never zeen a mimer do zat ztormy wind or glaz door zing before, George. You are a *genius*.'

'Oh, I wouldn't go that far, Roland,' I say modestly. '*Gifted* is the word my mother sewed onto my underpants.'

Our cabin is large but filled with racks of costumes and boxes of props for the various onboard shows. I see Amy has just destroyed a rubber rabbit that was in a top hat.

'What did you think of Roland, Izzy?' Chase asks.

Isobel sits on her bed. She looks exhausted.

'Don't,' she whispers, 'trust him.'

'Exactly.' Chase nods. 'He's dodgy as hell.'

The *Titania*'s horn blows loudly. I feel the ship lurch, then oh-so-slowly she begins to move!

'Well,' Chase says. 'No getting off now. Next stop, *Mayonnaise*, France!'

It will take us a few days to get to the city of Marseilles, so we are stuck with Roland, who does seem a little untrustworthy. But most importantly at this moment, Isobel should rest. So I suggest she sleeps while Chase and I check out the ship. We leave, making sure to lock the cabin door.

'I bet Roland knows about the reward,' Chase says, looking at the water surging wildly along the ship's side. 'He'll hand us over to the bad guys in an instant for cash.'

Being in New York City has taught me one thing about the power of money. And that is if you lose it, you want it back. And the more you've lost, the more you want it.

'We'll keep one step ahead,' I say, as we stop near the ship's hairdressing salon. 'And take *appropriate* action when required.'

'What do you mean by *appropriate?*' Chase asks.

'I don't know,' I answer. 'But I'm getting my *inappropriate* haircut sorted out right now!' And into the hairdressing salon I go.

I sit in front of the mirror in Pierre's Hair-We-Are-At-Sea Salon.

'This *thing*,' says Pierre, holding up a hank of my light brown hair, 'has to go right back to ground zero. It is making me a little tiny bit ill . . .'

'Yes, it's a style that doesn't suit,' I agree, if not quite to the same extent. 'Short back and sides for me, thanks, Pierre.'

With a swirl of his black cape, Pierre switches on a pair of red clippers.

'Do not move, George,' he says. 'These things are deadly!'

I shut my eyes, which turns out to be a mistake.

'Stage One,' Pierre announces two minutes later, 'is complete!'

I open my eyes and see that I have nothing but a strip of hair running right over the top of my head. It's a spiky Mohawk!

'Pierre,' I say, 'I am not a Mohawk person. I have no official ties to that fine North American people renowned for ferocity, porcupine quill artworks, and the ability to work at heights. You'll have to fix this!'

Pierre waves a pink comb. 'Relax, George—'

Bells start ringing and keep on ringing. Pierre swaps his comb for a hair dryer.

'We're sinking, George! Take *only* the essentials!' He runs for the door. 'Hurry! Women, children, and hairdressers first!'

'It's only a practice drill,' I say, not moving. 'Just fix my hair, Pierre. Then we'll go.'

But Pierre has gone, leaving me to think that if the ship doesn't sink, this haircut could still mean the end of me.

CHAPTER TWENTY-TWO

After the lifeboat drill is over, I go back to the salon with Chase. There's a 'Closed' notice on the window and the lace curtains are drawn. Chase laughs.

'Now you're stuffed, Georgie-boy.'

'Very funny, Chase,' I say. 'Imagine if I meet a Mohawk chief who thinks I've turned a traditional hairstyle into a flippant fashion statement?'

'You look forty per cent tougher,' Chase adds.

'I don't want to look tough,' I say. 'I want to look like George Parker, a chess player interested in astronomy, who immerses himself up to the eyeballs in education and algae. That's green algae, Chase, *green*. Red algae is overrated and I won't hear another word about it.'

We return to the cabin to see Isobel is still asleep.

'I am happy,' she murmurs drowsily. 'Happy.'

Well, that's good news.

'Isobel speaks French,' Chase informs me. 'At least, she did before the accident. It might come in handy, since we're going to France.'

'I also have a basic knowledge of the language,' I inform Chase. 'The French word for algae is *algue. Algue vert et algue rouge.* Green algae and red algae. You don't want to get the two mixed up, I can assure you, no sirree.'

'Anyway, moving on,' says Chase. 'It's dinnertime. And as we are *actors*, we have our own table.'

Isobel sleeps on peacefully. 'Perhaps we'll bring her something back?' I suggest. 'And let her rest.'

'Good thinking,' says Chase. 'We'll leave Amy on guard. Come on, let's go.'

We leave, locking the door, and walk up the tilting deck. Shrouded lifeboats hang over us and the sea hisses, reminding me that it's dangerous to be out on the deep dark ocean if you have enemies, because there's nowhere to go except overboard.

Chase and I sit at a table with the other entertainers. Beside Roland are two muscular ladies in grey overalls eating steak. He introduces them as Olga and Katerina, from Murmansk in Russia.

'Zey are vairy fonny twin acrobatz,' he adds. 'So fonny and zweet. Like liddle daffodil flowerz or luffly budderfliez.'

Katerina and Olga stare with cold grey eyes. Daffodils? Butterflies? Funny? Somehow I can't see them sharing a rib-tickling riddle or a fascinating fun fact about the discovery of gold in 1854 to brighten up a damp afternoon polishing chess pieces down at Chargers HQ.

'I believe Murmansk has the northern-most trolley bus system in the world,' I say cheerfully.

'Shut up about trolley bus,' says Katerina sourly.

'Your haircut,' says Olga. 'Stoopid.'

I'd forgotten about my Mohawk. I look around the dining room for Pierre, but there's no sign – nor any sign of Mohawks, either, which is a relief, because I doubt I could whip up a porcupine quill artwork if asked, and that's not only because removing quills from a porcupine would be best left to the experts.

'My haircut was totally accidental,' I offer. 'But I dedicate it to the Mohawk nation, a people proudly represented in Canada *and* the USA, whose culture remains strong and vibrant to this day.'

'Zat 'aircut iz boring me to bitz, Gheorge.' Roland picks his yellow teeth with a steel toothpick. 'But zpicking of bitz, tomorrow night I will zaw you in 'alf in my magic zhow and ze piezes of Gheorge will dizappear and everybotty vill zink vairy fonny.'

'Not everybody,' I say. 'Especially if I don't reappear, Roland. Certainly not from the point of view of my forward-thinking parents who have already pre-purchased my school shoes and extended my single bed by six centimetres in the not-unlikely expectation that I might grow.'

'Oh, *truzt* me.' Roland pats his heart. 'Ant Chaze, you will do dangerouz ztunt wiz lovely twinkle toez Olga and zlender fairy prinzezz Katerina.'

Chase laughs merrily. 'I do love a dangerous stunt, Roland! Now dear George, I think I left the iron on. Perhaps you'd better pop back and check?'

I leave the dining room and walk down the deserted deck. Once in the cabin, I see Isobel sitting up with her sketchbook. She shows me a beautiful picture of the Landon-Bond mansion, with a 'For Sale' sign on it.

'Our family,' she whispers. 'In serious trouble.'

'Yes,' I say. 'But I'm sure it'll all work out fine in the end.'

I hope so, because there's nothing worse than a tragic ending when I might be part of it.

I'm heading back along the deck when a masked figure in a black velvet cape drops down like a spider. Pierre!

'You need to fix my haircut, Pierre,' I say. 'I am not a Mohawk person. This style totally misleads and misrepresents my cultural values and sensitivities to other peoples from around the globe.'

'No can do, my friend.' Pierre adjusts a smiley-face button on his shirt. 'Pierre *never* goes back to a haircut. But George, I heard Roland the Magician tell Katerina and Olga that he is going to hand you over to some people in France. For a *stupendously* large reward.'

Good lord! 'Oh, he's making stuff up,' I tell Pierre. 'After all, he is a magician.'

'Is he?' Suddenly Pierre sets off, climbing upwards towards the next deck like a gymnast, although the stairs are only round the corner. His pointy-chinned, pale face looks down. 'Take care, George! And come in for a complimentary wash and blow-wave any time you like!'

After dinner, Chase and I discuss how we'll deal with what Roland has planned.

'He's a dirty double-crosser,' I say. 'And dirty double-crossers deserve to be double-crossed before they can double-cross the double-*crossees*. Which is us.'

'*Correct*,' says Chase. 'And here's how we'll outsmart him.' He leans forward. 'We go along with his stupid show, then whoosh! We make a break for Paris! Then straight back to Australia, our home that is girt by sea!'

'Although I do appreciate the reference to our wonderful national anthem, Chase,' I say, 'your plan seems a little *light* on detail.'

'Nonsense,' he answers and winks. 'It's perfect.'

CHAPTER TWENTY-THREE

We take Isobel to breakfast in a quiet dining room called the View of the Back of the Ship Restaurant. Behind us, the *Titania*'s wake widens like a white road on a blue landscape – or seascape, in this case.

'I prefer to see where I'm going,' Chase says, 'than where I've been.'

'Looking backwards, philosophically,' I counter, 'hopefully stops you repeating mistakes made in the past, Chase. Theoretically speaking, that is. Although it's not recommended while riding a bicycle or a horse, for example.'

'Yeah, nah, whatever,' says Chase.

'Our dad,' Isobel murmurs, 'should think about the past *and* the future a little bit more.'

'Well, that is a point, Izzy.' Chase nods wisely. 'Yep, I sure hope the old boy won't lose another couple of hundred million any time soon, as it makes life a bit difficult.'

A *bit*?

After breakfast, we go to the cabin, and Chase sets about looking through the various boxes, trunks, and cupboards.

'Check this out, Georgie.' He holds up a black semi-automatic assault rifle! 'Cool or what?'

'Guns!' I rush over and look in a trunk that's full of weapons. '*What* the—'

'They're *props*, George.' Chase hands me a grenade launcher. 'They're not real.'

'Oh, thank goodness,' I say, making sure not to point the grenade launcher at anything, which is impossible, as there is always something *everywhere*. 'They look real.'

'Which means they might come in very handy.' Chase picks up a revolver. 'Ka-blam! Blam! Blam!'

I'm not so sure about that, remembering a road-rage incident at kindergarten when one little chap on a tricycle pointed a plastic gun at another little chap in a pedal car, who ran off the road and straight through the front door of the cubby house where, fortunately, four children playing doctors and nurses applied first-aid using gumleaves and green cordial.

'Anyway, George,' Chase puts down the fake

weapon and shuts the trunk. 'It's time for rehearsals with our trusted friend, Roland.'

While Chase is being thrown around by Olga and Katerina, I spend my time in a coffin-like box on the stage.

'When I zaw zis box in 'alf, Gheorge,' Roland says, holding a long silver saw, 'you 'ave already dizzap-peared out ze hole in ze bottom like a zkaredy-cat ztinking rabbit.'

'Oh, I see, Roland,' I say. 'How very clever.'

Roland smiles, showing dirty teeth.

'It iz all an *illuzion*. Truzt me, Gheorge.'

I see another box at the back of the stage. It has a heavy-duty latch and handles welded to it.

'Zat zpare box,' Roland says, 'iz none of your biznezz, zticky beak Gheorge. Do not look at it wiz your eyez or anyzing elze.'

Chase comes over as Katerina and Olga take a drinks break, which they obviously need, as both are sweating like a pair of brewery draught horses.

'Oh, they're funny ladies.' Chase crosses his eyes. 'They laugh every time they drop me. Here.' Chase hands me his drink bottle. 'Drink.'

I do, although my mother says sharing bottles is as risky as knitting in bad light or boiling the kettle in bare feet.

'Go away, zticky beak Gheorge and zmarty panz Chaze,' Roland says. 'Zee you tonight.'

We go out onto the deck and breathe in the cool, clean ocean air. Far below, waves race by.

'Roland thinks he can deliver us to the bad dudes,' Chase says, 'like three little pigs off to market. Well, that's not gonna happen.'

I certainly hope not, as I'm aware that not many pigs that go to market ever go home or reach retirement age, except perhaps as aged bacon slices in long-life vacuum-sealed packs. Boy, I wish I was back at Tapley Grammar working on my simplified counting system that presently runs for about seven hundred pages. I would feel a *lot* safer.

CHAPTER TWENTY-FOUR

After dinner, we leave Isobel and Amy in the cabin and head to the ship's Entertainment Hub to perform in Master Roland's True Magic Show with Quite Difficult Acrobatics and Russian-Style Humour. As a rather accomplished amateur comedian myself, I feel that Olga and Katerina might struggle to get laughs, as they don't have one decent knock-knock joke between them, or any personality, either.

'What would Russian-style humour be, anyway?' I ask Chase, as I pull on a white dog suit with big brown spots. 'Perhaps it's just humour that's not supposed to be funny.'

'In that case,' Chase replies, dressing as an elf in green tights, a puffy red shirt, and a pointy hat, 'they'd be superstars.'

'Does this make my bottom look big?' I peer backwards. 'Hmmm, and my tail's droopy and some-what expressionless. I'm not sure I'll be totally believable as a reliable canine companion.'

'You're fine.' Chase pats my head. 'Good boy. Just remember not to talk, since dogs don't, as a rule.'

Olga and Katerina are putting on their make-up. They are wearing army camouflage leotards and have matching tattoos of tanks and flame-throwers on their biceps. Every so often, Katerina, the prettier one, spits on the floor.

'Completely hilarious,' Chase observes. 'Aren't they?'

Roland turns up in a black suit, brown shirt, orange bowtie, and black top hat.

'Firzt,' he says, 'Olga and Katerina do romantic Ruzzian folk danzing. Zen cometty acrobaticz wiz Chaze pixie-boy. Zen I zaw Gheorge in huff and disappear 'im totally. Finizh.'

'One problem,' I say, looking out through dog eyes. 'I can't stay disappeared.'

'Zilence!' Roland slaps my nose. 'Bat pippy dock! We ztart in two minutez!'

Chase and I wait backstage while Olga and Katerina act out a very violent scene from 'Little Red Riding Hood'. Roland stands by, holding a saw.

'That saw is real,' I whisper to Chase. 'What'll I do if something goes wrong?'

'Bark three times,' Chase suggests. 'I'll hear you.'

Good. That way I can stay in character *and* communicate, two important things for any dog actor whose life is in danger. I watch as Roland walks on stage.

'Now, laddiez and gentlemoonz,' he says, 'after zat luffly folkdance where ze woodcutterz chopz down Liddle Red Riding 'ood, luffly Olga and smoochy Katerina will be fonny wiz cheeky pixie boy, Chaze!'

'Good luck, Chase,' I say, as he springs onstage.

Olga and Katerina take Chase's arms and toss him towards the ceiling, catching him centimetres from the ground. This they do twice, the audience clapping.

'Now,' Roland gives a big dull-toothed smile, 'we 'ave 'ad 'igh, 'igher, and now ze 'ighezt!'

Katerina and Olga's muscles strain as they send Chase flying four or five metres into the air. Then they step apart, but Chase grabs a rope and swings overhead like a happy monkey. Roland is furious.

'Fall down, naughty bat boy Chaze!' He waves his cane wildly. 'You need *whack-whack* wiz magic ztick!'

The crowd clap, laugh and cheer.

'Bravo, Elf! Stay there, Pixie-boy! Bravo! Bravo!'

The clapping rolls on as Chase swings above the angry faces of Roland, Katerina, and Olga.

'Part One *finiz*,' Roland says angrily. He turns to a sailor named Nipper. 'Pull down ze curtain, *Nippair*.'

'Yes sir, yes sir.' Nipper hauls on a rope. 'Three bags full, sir.'

Olga and Katerina come backstage, followed by Roland, who's yelling at Chase.

'Everybotty laugh at uz! You 'it ze deck, zplat! Not 'ang upside down like movie hactor who zinks 'e is a bat, whatever 'is name iz.'

'Batman?' says Chase.

'Of course *not* Batman!' Roland's black eyes bulge. 'Now, Gheorge! Time I zaw you in 'alf zen you go up chimney, poof!'

Chimney? What chimney?

'Oh, that's a joke, Roland!' I hold my sides, shake and laugh, which is an advanced acting technique not many folk would know. 'Ho ho ho!'

'Get ratty, bat dock Gheorge!' He glares at Sailor Nipper. 'Ze curtain, Nippair!'

And up the green curtain goes.

CHAPTER TWENTY-FIVE

I dance around the box on my hind paws, which would suggest to the audience, I think, that I'm not a real dog.

'Danz, dizobedient docky, danz!' Roland swipes at me with his cane as the music speeds up. 'Danz, you pezky poppy!'

Every time he swings, I step back, and the crowd applauds harder and louder.

'Go, dog, go!' The crowd seems very involved. 'Go, dog, go!'

Roland throws open the lid of the box then picks up the saw.

'Ze bat zpotty dock muzt be zawn in 'alf!' He grabs me by the tail. 'Get in ze box, Gheorge, bat dock!'

I get in, the lid is shut, and I simply drop under the stage and sit there in the dark.

'Now we zay 'appy goot rittance to zat pezky poppy!'

Half an hour later, covered in sawdust, I'm let out by Roland.

'You zee, Gheorge?' He smiles that awful yellow smile. 'You can *truzt* Roland az if I am luffly polizeman or zuntanned zurf lifegart in Oztraylya.'

'Oh yes, I jolly well can trust you,' I say, using my recently acquired acting ability and talent for natural-sounding dialogue. 'Without one speckle of a doubt! You're just like my dear old scoutmaster, Trusty John McReliable!'

Using a realistic name that suggests trustworthiness, I think, has totally guaranteed that Roland doesn't suspect a thing. Boy, it seems I've inherited a talent for disguise like my great Canadian great-aunt, Aunt Selma Parker, who worked undercover as a female moose to capture illegal hunters until she was shot on the opening day of hunting season because she unfortunately put the wrong date in her calendar.

Oops!

CHAPTER TWENTY-SIX

The next two days pass quietly, although we're careful never to walk around the ship alone. This morning, I'm sitting on the sunny deck with Isobel, who is drawing.

'I can't go back to that hospital,' she whispers. 'Never ever.'

'No, you're going home,' I say, watching the waves rise and fall. 'It might take a while from France, Isobel. But we'll get there eventually.' *Hopefully*, I silently add.

She smiles. 'Paris is beautiful. We can stay on the barge.'

'That would be nice,' I say. 'I've never been on a barge.'

Isobel stops drawing. 'You're parents are scientists, aren't they, George? What kind of thing do they do exactly?'

'Well,' I answer. 'They're analysing moon rocks and other space material, hoping to discover things that will be useful on Earth.' Or valuable, although what my parents consider valuable might be very different to what Isobel's parents do. 'They try to solve world problems through science.'

Isobel smiles at me. 'That's what you do, too, in a way, George. I think it's wonderful.'

I blush. 'Well, thank you, Isobel. Maybe one day I might do something *really* useful. That's what I hope.'

At sunset, Chase and I sneak Amy up onto the exercise deck for a little walk.

'Wow,' Chase says. 'Being up here is like watching a movie of the world coming right at you.'

The *Titania* meets the black waves as she heads bravely towards the horizon as if it was the future. There is no sign of land, but I do see Pierre climbing down an emergency ladder, a royal-blue cape fluttering. He jumps, and lands sprawled like a clumsy cat.

'Pierre!' I help him up. 'I thought you'd vanished.'

'Me?' He swirls his cape. 'No, George, my salon is only open in the afternoons. In the mornings, I work in the ship's library.'

Well, that explains it.

'Anyway, peeps,' Pierre says. 'I must tell you that Roland was in the library researching the Great Houdini, the famous escape artist. He wanted to find out how many days you could safely lock people up in steel boxes without them suffocating.'

'And what did you say, Pierre?' Chase glances around the empty deck.

'I said, "Roland!"' Pierre puffs his chest out, '"that's *dangerous*."'

'And what did he say?' I ask.

Pierre shrugs. 'He said, "Not my problem."'

'Boy,' I say, '*so* unprofessional.'

'Anyway,' Pierre is poised to climb. 'If you're in trouble, you can always rely on a hairdresser or librarian. And I am both!' He climbs out of sight.

'He could've taken the stairs,' says Chase.

If I may say so, I think I understand Pierre a little better than Chase.

'Pierre is a risk-taking librarian-hairdresser,' I say. 'The fact that he wears a cape in public takes a lot of courage, Chase. I wouldn't feel *comfortable* wearing one, I can tell you.'

Chase picks up Amy. He's laughing, although I am *extremely* serious. Yes, it's true that it's often George Parker who cheers up a chap down at the Tapley

Chargers who has a wobbly chair leg, or is struggling with the lid of his lunchbox, but I'm not joking now.

'Pierre's cape,' I continue, 'is an expression of his colourful personality and daring dress sense. The cape actually *gives* him courage.'

'Okay,' Chase counters. 'Why don't army guys wear capes, then? A cape would help them out considerably, according to *your* theory.'

Chase's tone has rather got my goat, if I had a goat, which I don't. It's just an expression.

'Well!' I squiggle a finger in the air, as though writing. 'If you contacted the heads of our defence forces by letter or email,' I answer, 'and outlined my theory, you'd get a jolly good reception, Chase. A healthy self-image equals better results. For certain professions, a cape would work wonders. Although for helicopter pilots and such, I would suggest one with a weighted hem or an industrial-strength clothes-peg arrangement.'

Chase puts his arm around my shoulders. '*Mate*,' he says, 'you are the best kid in the world!'

The only time anyone has ever called me 'mate' was when a fellow yelled, '*Mate*, what the *heck* are you lookin' at!' I put that down to my short-sightedness, which can cause problems. At the zoo, I once mistook a large lady in a brown dress for an escaped American bison and called the keeper, resulting in an unpleasant moment or two.

'Well, *mate*,' I say, 'you're not a bad ...*dude* ... yourself!'

We leave the deck, knowing it's time to plan for tomorrow night's final show and how we will escape from Roland and the ship.

Isobel listens carefully. 'I can help,' she says.

Chase nods. 'Yes, if we need you, Izzy. But George and I have everything under control.'

Do we?

Isobel nods. 'I'll be in the audience. In case of an emergency.'

'Okay, but don't do anything mad,' Chase warns. 'You being trapped in a steel box won't do any of us any good.'

I'll second that.

CHAPTER TWENTY-SEVEN

Chase and I head to the Entertainment Hub for our final performance. I'm wearing an English highwayman's outfit, featuring black britches, a ruffled white shirt, a three-cornered hat, and a *cape,* which certainly does make me feel rather dashing. Chase is dressed as Shirley Temple, a famous child movie star with curly blonde hair who could sing and dance.

'Roland would never lock a little blonde girl in a steel box,' Chase explains as we wait backstage. 'Although he'd probably get away with locking up a highwayman. They used to hang them in the old days, George. A noose around the old neck, and see ya later, alligator! *Skurrrk!*'

I wonder if I have time to change?

Too late! Roland approaches.

'Oh, 'oo do I zee,' he says, clasping his pale hairy hands, 'but zat liddle zinging-danzing zuperztar, Zhirley Temple! Ant alzo zat dirty Ingliz 'ighway robbair, dizguzting, 'orrible Dick Turpin! Ah, my luffly actor chumz. What a night I 'ave planned for you!'

Oh, I bet you have, *Roland*! But I certainly know plans don't always work out perfectly. For example, after taking one wrong turn on a Sunday outing, the Parker family spent a rather long day at the world-class Werribee Sewage Farm instead of the world-class Werribee Free Range Zoo – a weekend that certainly has had me thinking every time I've flushed a toilet for the last seven years.

After Olga and Katerina have performed feats of strength, including smashing concrete blocks with sledge hammers, Roland stands centre-stage.

'Now,' he announces, 'liddle Zhirley-Chaze will zing, 'On ze Goot Zhip Lollypop', zen Roland will fight a duel wiz dirty, 'orrible monkey-looking Ingliz 'ighway robbair, Dick Gheorge Turpin-Parkair! And zhen zat dirty robbair zcoundrel will pay for 'is 'orrible crimez in a zteel box, nevair to be zeen again!'

Roland comes offstage. 'Truzt me, little Gheorge.' He puts a sweaty hand on my knee. 'Uncle Roland zez to you, zere'z no 'appy biznezz like zhow biznezz!'

He gives a song sheet to Chase. 'Your zong, Zhirly-Chaze! You are zinging zoon, zo get ratty!'

Olga and Katerina bow, then walk offstage, leaving a trail of perspiration. As Nipper brings the curtain down for interval, Olga stomps over in paratrooper boots and stands on the toes of my pointy black buckle-up shoes.

'Stupit robber, dirty Dick.' She pokes me with a finger like the handle of a hammer. 'Soon you go in steel box. Very fonny to lock you up like feelthy rat-traitor-cheating-shoplifter!'

I swirl my cape, fearless – *almost*. 'I am George Dick Turpin-Parker! And no one ever gets the better of Dick!' Well, that was until he was arrested then executed at the Tower of London, but that's another story.

'Ha!' Olga spits on my shoes. 'In my country, you go to Siberian salt mines with horrible, terrible, unattractive Siberian salt miners.'

'I'm sure all the Siberian salt miners,' I reply, 'in the audience would love to hear you say that. Not!'

'What is thees *not*?' Olga glares at me. 'That does not make sense, thees *not*, you hiding-in-the-bushes-stealing-ladies-underclothes-filthy-stagecoach-stopper!'

'I fling your insults far behind me,' I say, swirling my cape as I leave. 'Ha!'

While Roland bangs away at the piano, Chase Shirley Landon-Bond-Temple performs 'On the Good Ship Lollipop'.

'Now tap-danz, Zhirley-Chaze!' Roland yells. 'You muzt danze tapz, or I zpank you wiz magic sztick!'

Chase cannot tap-dance, so it's dashing George Dick Turpin-Parker to the rescue! I grab a rope, climb onto a table, and swing onstage with my cape streaming behind me. And when I hit the floor, I tap-dance *furiously*, my shiny black shoes cracking like duelling pistols every time I take a step.

SMACK! SMACK! SMACK! A-TAPPETY-TAP-TAP-TAP! And A-CRACKETY-CRACK-CRACK-CRACK!

The applause is loud, but Roland is furious.

'You zteal zhow from Chaze-Zhirley!' Roland advances, carrying two swords. 'Defend yourzelf, runaway-from-bathtime-dirty George Dick, you big fat stage 'og!' He throws me a sword.

I catch the shining silver weapon and leap onto the piano. Up I jump as Roland swipes at my feet.

'Missed!' I swipe back. 'Take that, you smelly magician and irresponsible illusionist!'

Roland lunges but I leap again, my cape like a falcon's wing.

Slash! Slash! Roland keeps on coming.

'Your black 'at,' he yells, ''az too many cornairs!'

'How dare you insult my hat!' I advance, but am grabbed from behind by four iron-like hands that must belong to Olga and Katerina.

'Zer magic steel box for you!' Katerina pushes me behind the curtain. 'You are dog meat now, dirty smuggler-of-stolen-treasure-and-probably-naughty-photos-of-Olga-and-Katerina-in sauna! Goodbye, and good rittance!'

At this point, everything goes black, and rather alarmingly, I see the magic box has no ventilation or inside latch. I now wish I was back at school. Again.

'George.'

I hear a quiet voice.

'Are you in that box?'

'Yes,' I say. 'Apparently.'

It's a great relief when the lid lifts. It's also quite a surprise to see that it's a nun in a habit who has given me my freedom.

'Thank you, Sister,' I say. 'That's very kind of you. Are you enjoying the cruise?'

The nun lifts off her headwear. 'It's me, George. Isobel! I found this outfit in our cabin.'

'Isobel!' I climb out of the box, seeing that my flounces have been flattened and my ruffles wrecked. 'You're a hero!'

'Chase is keeping a lookout in the passageway,' she whispers. 'Let's go.'

I have an idea. 'Wait.' I pick up bits of wood and some rags and put them into the box. 'Roland will think I'm still inside.' Then we shut the box and leave, joining Chase and moving quickly along a corridor that seems to be deep down inside the ship.

'Good to see you, George.' Chase is still dressed as Shirley Temple. 'Luckily, Sister Isobel followed the box because Roland kept me in the Entertainment Hub until Olga and Katerina had taken it away.'

We make it onto our deck, check that the coast is clear, then scamper back to our cabin and lock the door.

'I'll be glad to get off this old tub tomorrow.' Chase lies in his bunk. 'I'll feel a lot safer in Paris. Then we can see if it's okay for Isobel to fly home.'

I agree, as my affection for magic shows, tap-dancing, and ship-board life has been stretched to breaking point.

'How's the money situation, Chase?' I ask hopefully.

He shakes his head. 'Hard to tell, Georgie. My dad has cut off all communications to avoid being tracked down and now he's gone off yachting somewhere.' Chase sighs. 'You'd think these other guys'd just let the whole thing go. It's not as if it hasn't happened before.'

I can see why these people might *not* want to let it go *completely*.

'We can't just walk off the ship with everyone else,' I say. 'We'd be grabbed in an instant. There has to be another way.'

'For a start, George,' Chase says, 'we'll go in disguise. That's been working quite well for us. Then you can think of something else. It doesn't matter if it's a bit risky. Who cares?'

Well, I do, for one.

'No, Chase,' Isobel whispers. 'George has already been so brave.'

Have I? I thought I'd been exceptionally scared most of the time, because it's a fact that the Parkers are more fearful than fearless.

'I'll sleep on it,' I say. 'And in the morning, I'm sure I'll be *full* of ideas.'

Isobel smiles. 'Soon, we'll be in Paris.'

Quite frankly, I'd prefer to be back in my room at Tapley, working on my Smart Bath Mat with internet connection and global roaming, which I'm quite sure will be a big player in the shared-bathroom-equipment-for-the-elderly economy of the future.

'Anyway, George,' says Chase, 'your Mohawk's coming along nicely. Very punk rock.'

'In no way,' I say, 'am I a punk rocker, Chase. The music scares me. And the way they misuse safety pins and buttons is just asking for trouble.'

Chase rummages through a box and comes up with a tatty, sleeveless denim jacket with a Union Jack flag sewn on the back. It smells atrocious.

'But *what* a disguise, George!' He tosses it to me. 'It's *perfect*. You can be really rude and spit all over the place, because that's what punks do. It'll be fun for you!'

'Rudeness is *not* the way a normal person has fun, Chase,' I say. 'And I'm not a spitter, either. For one thing, I have a gap between my front teeth. And the idea of *practising* to be a spitter isn't something I'd leap at.'

Chase laughs as he throws me some terrible jeans and silly purple boots.

'I'm sure you'll discover hidden talents.'

'Neither spitting nor being rude are talents,' I reply sternly. 'And I can't see why these jeans are held together with pins and chains. Bulldog clips would've been a far safer option. Though it's possible they might pinch, and I encountered enough pinchers at primary school to last a lifetime – which averages more than eighty years, Chase, according to the Australian Bureau of Statistics.'

Isobel, I see, looks rather worried.

'Oh, I'll be *fine*, Isobel,' I say reassuringly. 'I recently completed a one-hour online self-defence course and answered all questions correctly, including some rather complex colouring in. I'm stronger than I look,' I add. 'I often do ten to fifteen push-ups a week. And recently, I've had a number of Final Five finishes in Poison Ball.'

I see Chase has picked out a khaki French Foreign Legion soldier's uniform.

'I *like* this,' he says. 'Check the hat, Georgie-boy.'

I have serious doubts about Chase's latest disguise.

'I'm not sure you should pretend to be a Foreign Legionnaire in France,' I suggest. 'Because you'd be expected to speak French. And you can't.'

Chase holds up a pale green shirt with lots of patches and medals.

'I'll just speak English with a French accent,' he says. 'Or be the strong silent type. That would be a Foreign Legion thing, I'd reckon.'

I look at us: me, a punk rocker with glasses, Isobel as an exceedingly young nun, and Chase, a French Foreign Legionnaire unable to obey orders or even direct a lost tank onto the right road – or *rue*, as a street is called in France.

'This is not a game,' I inform Chase, and Amy, in case she's listening. 'Getting off this ship will be a life-threatening situation.'

Chase is now trying on a pair of lace-up combat boots. 'Right you are, George. What did you say?'

'Oh, ask Amy.' I'm rather annoyed. 'I'm going to clean my teeth.' Clara, my dental hygienist, would be appalled at my lack of flossing lately. She's unbending in her belief that rinsing is no substitute and eating an apple just leads to a false sense of security.

I stop at the bathroom door and see that Chase is now wearing the full French Foreign Legion outfit.

'Anyway, Georgie,' he says, 'punks are supposed to have dirty teeth. Yep, filthy fangs, mouldy molars, and putrid pegs! Say ta-ta to the Tooth Fairy, GP! You're gonna have breath like a blue-tongued lizard.'

This time Chase has gone too far!

'I'm risking enough trying to get off this ship,' I fire back, 'without letting myself in for a filling or setting the foundations for gum disease later in life. I'm no thrill-seeker in the dental department, no sir. I'm like a beaver in that regard, Chase. You can take it from me that our furry friends know the value of good strong teeth!' I shut the bathroom door firmly against Chase's grinning face. 'Thank goodness for fluoride,' I murmur to myself. 'That's all I can say.'

CHAPTER
TWENTY-EIGHT

The next morning, we have a quick breakfast and then put on our disguises. The *Titania* is due to dock at 10 a.m. in Marseilles, a port in the south of France.

'Perhaps,' I say, 'as we're in disguise, we could just casually go down the gangplank with everyone else? Because sometimes—'

A key grinds in our door. *What?!*

'You can't come in,' I call out. 'I'm folding my underwear and my companions are doing a crossword. They're currently stuck on a seven-letter word that starts with B and ends in D ... a medicinal dressing applied to a minor wound—'

The door flings inwards and two big men in black overalls and black masks come storming in. They are wearing packs and carrying rolls of masking tape and a coil of rope!

'Da word is *bandaid*,' the biggest man spits out. 'And you'll need a 'undred of 'em if you don't come quietly. Because dis game of charades is *over*.'

We're cornered! The leader turns to me.

'Do anyfink clever, punky-boy, and you'll be one dead duck.'

The situation is desperate, so I reach into a box, take out one of the fake guns that has a silencer on it, and aim it at the gentleman in black. Boy, it's rather heavy for recycled plastic.

'We're leaving,' I say. 'Get in the bathroom, or it'll be you needing the bandaids, sirs. And if you think they're difficult to get out of the packet now, just try it when you're full of bullet holes.'

The big guys stop, giving Chase the chance to grab our backpacks and push Isobel towards the door.

'Into the bathroom, thank you,' I repeat, with concrete *and* ice in my voice. 'Or I'll—'

The big guy steps towards me. 'Or whot, snotty boy?'

Tzit! Tzit! Tzit! Tzit! Pzeeow, pzeeow, pzeeow, pzeeow!

The gun kicks and bullets buzz around the cabin like enraged bees! Holy pyjama party! The damn thing's real! And I see, when the smoke clears, that the two monsters have jumped into the bathroom and shut the door, which I simply lock before stepping out on the deck, turning the key in the cabin door then dropping it and the gun into the ocean.

'Bravo, Georgie-boy,' Chase says as we walk away as though nothing has happened. 'Wow! You're a real gunfighter.'

I am shaking. 'You said those things weren't real.'

He shrugs as we look for a place to keep safely out of the way.

'I didn't go through them *all*,' he says. 'Anyway, no harm done, so it's fun, fun, fun!'

I'm about to disagree in the strongest terms when a caped figure drops from a lifeboat. It's Pierre, wearing ballet shoes and holding a stack of books.

'Come with me, chaps!' He tucks the books under one arm. 'Roland's searching every deck. But I have a *lovely* plan!'

We follow Pierre into a service lift that delivers us down into a huge open space that smells of oil and echoes with deafening clangs and bangs as metal hits metal and things grind and grate. I see there are dumpsters filled with bulging rubbish bags and one that is half-filled with books.

'I'm spring-cleaning the library,' Pierre explains. 'Once I've read the books, I just send them away and get new ones. It's a good system.'

If anyone cares to look, they will see my self-tracking safety wallet *bulges* with library cards collected over a lifetime. So when it comes to library operations, I would modestly call myself something of an expert.

'But *other* people,' I suggest to Pierre, 'might want to read the books, mightn't they?'

Pierre drops the books into the container. 'They had their chance, George. It's not my job to make sure that the damn things are borrowed.'

I would heartily disagree, but I reluctantly leave the discussion of the librarian's role in modern society for another day.

'What's your plan, Pierre?'

Pierre points. 'You hide in there with the books. And although it'll be a bit dark to read once the lid's locked, the box will be taken off the ship sometime this morning. Then you simply walk away when the container arrives wherever it's supposed to arrive at.'

'Which is where, Pierre?' I ask.

Pierre considers. 'Somewhere, I suppose.'

'More information,' says Chase. 'Please.'

'France?' Pierre's eyebrows go down. 'I don't know. Where do old books go? The shredder? Back to the idiots who wrote them?'

'I'm not getting into that box.' Isobel shakes her head.

I'm not keen on being put through a shredder by an illiterate French person with no regard for printed or human matter, either.

'Perhaps,' Pierre says, 'you could use the gangway that the crew uses. Although you don't look like sailors.'

I pat Pierre on the back. 'That's a *wonderful* idea.'

Chase looks around. 'Pierre, can we grab some of those overalls hanging up over there? It'll be like borrowing library books, except that they might not be returned.'

Pierre looks confused. 'Are library books supposed to come back? Really? I just thought it was people being annoying. But yes, take the overalls. Although that *dark* green colour would only suit the dullest of types. *Green*? Yuk schmuck! Dreadful colours for dreadful people, that's what I say.'

Well, *I* was about say that I quite *like* the dark green, but I won't now.

Chase goes to the rack and takes down three pairs of overalls. 'You've saved the day, Pierre. And I'd like to give you a little cash reward.'

'Oh, no, Chase. I don't want money.' Pierre wags a pink finger. 'I only wish to help. Besides, my leotards have no pockets, and I don't want to poke it anywhere that might scratch.' He backs away. 'Travel safe, dear friends. Bye-bye.' And slowly he climbs up a steel grating and out of sight.

'If only everybody in the world was that good,' says Isobel.

'But they're not.' Chase puts his white Foreign Legion hat into his bag, but leaves his Shirley Temple wig on. 'Let's get cracking. Because this next bit's going to be tricky.'

CHAPTER TWENTY-NINE

So, dressed as grubby sailors, we hide behind the last dumpster in the line as the ship edges into the dock. There's lots of shouting, the whirring of electric motors, and chains dragging as the *Titania* settles, her engines humming gently.

'We're in France,' Chase says. 'Almost.'

There's a loud screeching sound and daylight shines into the ship's hold. They're lowering a ramp to conduct 'roll-on roll-off loading', where containers are used to re-supply the ship and remove what has been used on the voyage.

'I'm taking a peek,' says Chase, and climbs a steel ladder. 'Yep, it's all happening,' he calls down. 'Plenty of opportunity to get squashed, I'll say that much.'

Isobel covers her ears. 'Noise hurts my head.'

I'm sure all this banging and crashing is not helping Isobel at all. So I open my backpack and take out a woollen beanie that my mother knitted in the Tapley colours. The chess-playing lads at the

Chargers preferred a balaclava, but Mister Ponce-Jones, our tactical advisor, thought that some of the more sensitive boys might scare themselves if they looked in a mirror.

'This will help.' I hold it out. 'And you'll look more like a sailor.'

Chase climbs down. 'There's a walkway beside the ramp. I say we give it a go. Let's roll.'

'Right.' I pick up my pack and push Amy's warm little head down. 'Let's just stroll on down and if anyone says anything, just nod and keep on going. Agree?'

We agree and set off towards . . . France!

The ramp to the wharf is like a metal road with a separate walkway. People are coming and going, so we simply follow a large crewman and hope for the best.

'*Bonjour*,' says a seaman coming the other way, carrying an enormous spanner.

'*Bonjour*,' says another fellow.

'*Bonjour, bonjour, bonjour!*' Everyone's saying it, coming and going. '*Bonjour!*'

So we start saying it as well.

'*Bonjour*,' I say. '*Bonjour*.' I say it to anyone who is close enough to hear. '*Bonjour, bonjour, bonjour!*'

Chase takes it a step further. He waves, makes little bows, gives the thumbs-up, and is generally the friendliest French seaman on this side of the Atlantic Ocean.

'*Bonjour! Bon-jour! Oui, bonjour!* Ah, *bonjour!* Eh, *bonjour! Bon-jour-jour-jour!*'

Isobel quietly walks right behind the chap in front, and then we are off the ramp. But unfortunately, there's an enormous man in white overalls and black wrap-around glasses blocking our way.

'Oi.' He points with a blunt finger. 'Have youse Frenchies seen two boys and a girl gettin' orf dis ship? Dey are wanted for crimez against 'umanity. Or somefin' awful, anyway.'

'*Non*,' I answer, and delve deeply into my bag of acting tricks. 'I 'ave no English, madam. We air French. *Pardon. Au revoir! Pardon!*'

'*Oui*,' says Chase. 'No Eenglish for me eezer, but zee cat zets on ze mat and iz zo 'appy 'az no pippy docks barkz at 'im! Goodbye, sweetie-pie.'

Isobel just shrugs in what appears to be a very French way.

'Oh, go away den,' says the giant. 'Yore accentz iz givin' me a terrible 'eadache.'

Our accents? What a damned cheeky chap! But I say nothing, and then, just as we're almost safely past, Amy barks quite loudly from inside my backpack.

Woof!

The giant spins around and reaches inside his overalls!

'Whot woz that?'

'*Pardonez-moi!*' I start spluttering. 'I 'ave ze 'orrible zicknezz from tropical pigz. Zis zicknezz zitz in le stomach for evair. Wiz zome zmelly gaz. Well, a lot of zmelly gaz. No more girlfrienz for me! Nevair evair evair!'

Woof! Woof! Woof!

I splutter some more.

The big man backs away, holding a little white lace handkerchief to his face.

'Go! Get! Be off with yer, you 'orrible liddle man!'

We don't hang around. We quickly climb two flights of stairs, walk down a long corridor, walk around three corners, and suddenly we're in the city of Marseilles!

'Lose the overalls, everyone,' Chase says. 'Take them off behind that big sign there.'

We sneak behind a sign that declares that people without proper documentation will be put in jail, and stroll out again as a punk rocker, a delicate nun, and a dashing French Foreign Legionnaire who have illegally entered France. Then we swap American dollars for euros and take a taxi to Saint-Charles Station. *Easy.*

Next stop, gay Paris!

Inside the old station, we study a flickering electronic timetable and work out that we have eleven minutes to buy tickets and catch the train to Paris. Chase hands me money.

'Best if I don't talk, George,' he says, 'as my French is not quite up to scratch. You'd better buy the tickets. Good luck.'

Isobel signals that I should come close. '*Trois billets pour Paris*, George,' she murmurs. '*S'il vous plait.* Okay?'

Not feeling very confident, I walk towards the ticket office and repeat the phrase. Yet it all goes surprisingly smoothly, not because I speak French but because the lady speaks English!

Jolly good show!

CHAPTER THIRTY

We get onto a silver space-age train that has wonderful seats and big wide windows. I was worried about smuggling Amy on board, but in our carriage alone I count three poodles, two wearing velvet jackets and one a little red hat. So I settle back and sneer, Chase ignores everyone, and Isobel sits with her hands in her lap, looking like the perfect nun should look – perfect.

'Check this out, Georgie-boy.' Chase shows me a text from his dad as we speed through the French countryside, which appears to be quite dry and rocky.

Found fifty million I'd forgotten. Still short a couple of hundred. Nice weather. How's school?

How could you forget where *fifty million dollars* was?

'What did you say about that?' I whisper.

Chase shrugs. 'I said school was great. That's what he likes to hear.'

'No,' I whisper. 'About the money? Wouldn't fifty

million calm these people down? Like a deposit until your dad can come up with the rest?'

Before Chase can answer, I see two tough-looking ticket inspectors who remind me of Olga and Katerina, and a third who looks remarkably like Roland enter our carriage. Oh, no!

'We've got trouble,' I whisper to Chase and Isobel. 'Get your tickets out quick. And act normal.'

'What sort of *normal*?' Chase asks. 'French normal? English normal? Australian normal? All or none of the above?'

'Just *normal* normal.' I shrug. 'Just not *ab*-normal.'

Before I can clarify things, Roland arrives, and asks in French for our tickets, presumably. So we hold them up, he checks them over, and hands them back.

'*Merci*,' he says slowly, peering at us as if he's trying to see into our souls.

'Yeah, dat's it, mate, fanks,' I say, punk-rocker-style. Isobel nods gently, and Chase salutes . . . and Roland continues on, turning twice to look back.

Whew!

But now Olga and Katerina are closing in. Suddenly Katerina stops, pinches my cheek really hard, and stares into my face like a cobra that's just had its tail slammed in a door.

183

'You remind lovely Katerina of someone bad vit' stoopid haircut, naughty punk dirty-denim-probably-no-underpants safety-pin boy. Vot your name?'

Don't say George, I tell myself, trying not to panic.

'Elizabeth!' I blurt. '*Bert,* I mean,' I add. 'Yeah, Bert. Urghh.'

Katerina pokes me in the chest. 'You better be Bert, not Eliza-bert. Katerina keep eyes on you, rocker-boy. Also, I think I smell you before. Somevere else.'

Me? Smell?

'Oh, I just ate me like a big bucket of snails,' I say. 'Yer know? Dem slimy fings in shells. Disgustin', they woz! Ooh, lovely!'

'You not French.' Katerina stares at me. 'Vy eat snail? No one eat snail except for maybe Siberian salt miners who eat anyzing goink, including bugs and stickz and vood plankz.'

'I ate snails,' I say, 'because I was hungry. Not all punk rockers spit everything out, you know.'

Katerina flicks my safety pins. 'I vould like send you to Siberian salt mine, living in unpleasant Siberian village with unpleasant Siberians. Teach you a lesson. Those Siberians bash you up and down, both vays.'

I can no longer restrain myself. 'If you visit Siberia,' I say, 'you might be pleasantly surprised at the price of salt, and how nice the Siberians are. I believe their local handcrafts are exceptional.'

Katerina scowls. 'Katerina remembers! You remind her of zneaky scoundrel George Dirty Dick Turpin-Parker! A stinking bad boy even vorse than you!' Then she walks on, banging the side of my head with a bottom like the boot of a car.

Then she's gone, and I let go a sigh of utter relief.

'Look on the bright side, Georgie,' Chase whispers. 'This is an *adventure*. Who knows where we'll end up?'

That's certainly true. I just hope I'm alive to enjoy it when we get there.

Isobel touches my wrist. 'In Paris,' she whispers, 'we will disappear into the city. It will be like a dream.'

Isobel's calmness is reassuring. Yes, Paris is surely a huge city where we cannot be found.

'Imagine if we got stuck there for years,' says Chase cheerfully. 'We really might have to join the Foreign Legion. That'd be hilarious!'

I think it would be horrendous! Joining a foreign fighting force enforcing foreign policy forcefully on foreign people would be extremely foreign to any Parker person!

'Anything,' Isobel whispers, 'is possible.'

That's what I'm afraid of!

CHAPTER THIRTY-ONE

The train arrives at Gare de Lyon, a Paris railway station that is, of course, big and busy. People rush everywhere, the sounds of suitcases on wheels almost as loud as the trains arriving and departing.

'*Voilà!*' says Chase, spinning around. 'We're here. Paris! We're *free*. Let's hit the streets!'

We leave the station and walk out into the stunning golden city of Paris. It's sunny, cold, and exciting but I think it's most important that we make sure Isobel doesn't walk too far, although she looks as happy as I've ever seen her. And why not? Paris is known as the City of Light and light is good for plants, people, animals, reading in bed, and finding things inside a fridge.

'We need a place to stay,' I tell Chase. 'Isobel has to rest.'

Chase nods. 'Cheap or expensive, Georgie? Near the river or up a hill? Left bank or right bank? Modern or ancient? Funky or clunky?'

'Ask Isobel,' I suggest. 'She knows the city best.'

Isobel points. 'Let's go to the river Seine. It's wonderful.'

We cross the Seine on a beautiful stone bridge and find ourselves in a park with avenues of trees and paths surrounded by huge stone buildings.

'Trees!' Isobel walks to the closest and rests her cheek on the trunk, as if listening to its heartbeat. 'I love them.'

It starts to rain gently as we walk slowly through the gardens, Amy running around as dusk settles, Paris feeling like a city where the past seems to exist with the present. Leaving the gardens, we pass a tall, narrow building with golden lights shining behind little curtained windows. It is called L'Hotel Geranium.

'Here,' says Isobel. 'I like this place.'

So I stow Amy in my backpack, we go into an old foyer, and I tap on a little brass bell that goes *ping*! And out of a very small door comes a tiny old lady dressed in black.

'*Bon soir*,' she says from behind a vase of flowers that I suppose are geraniums. 'I 'ave a lovely room for you young people. It is vairy old, beautiful, and quiet.'

'*Parfait*,' says Isobel, and smiles. '*Merci, madame.*'

'You are welcome.' The little old lady hands Isobel a great big black key. 'Pay later, darlingz. Breakfazt include. Fair price.' Then the hotel manageress smiles what would be a toothy smile, if she had any teeth. 'You are actorz, *non*?'

Chase makes a little bow. 'In a way, yes.'

The little lady's bony hands circle in the air. 'Or are you in *dizguize*?'

'Perhaps a little bit of both,' I answer, feeling Amy squirming in my pack. 'But we have broken no laws, madame, I assure you.' This, I realise, is untrue. We've probably broken about five hundred.

The tiny lady motions that I should move closer, her face a maze of criss-crossing lines like a crinkled road map.

'When Vivienne was vairy young,' she whispers, 'I 'ide from ze Germans! I work in ze Resistance, *oui*? I keep secrets for *seventy-five* years.' She motions me even closer. I can smell mint, garlic, and tobacco. 'Vivienne bring you old cloze. And Colt .45 handgon. Or machine gon. Bayonet. Parachute. Boom. I mean, bomb.'

This is unexpected, that has to be said. 'Only clothes, please, Vivienne,' I say. 'We don't need any,

er, other things. No gons or booms. Guns and bombs, I mean.' I'm also thinking that a seventy-year-old parachute might prove to be something of a disappointment. 'But thank you.'

''Ow about some 'and grenades?' She sweeps back wisps of grey hair. 'I 'ave a little tank 'idden at my 'oliday house in the forest.'

'It's very kind of you, Vivienne,' I reply. 'At the moment I think we only need some clothes and for Isobel to rest.'

Vivienne studies Isobel. 'You need chicken zoup, zweetiepie. And an 'ug.' She steps from behind the counter and hugs Isobel. 'Now. Go upstairs, childrens. I bring zings.' Then Vivienne stands on tip-toes to unzip my backpack, and Amy pops her head out. 'And let ze little dog 'ave zome air!'

Our room has an ancient honey-coloured wooden floor that rises and falls in waves. Our single beds have thick white eiderdowns, and there's an oval mirror with strange dark patches that don't reflect anything. Outside, I can see pointy slate roofs like grey waves disappearing into the Paris night.

'This room is wonderful,' Isobel says, and does a

little waltz under a glass chandelier with much of the glass missing. 'So old and happy.'

The room feels like a hideaway from the modern world. I just wish we could relax and explore the city outside without the fear that Roland is hunting for us.

'Where is your barge, exactly?' I ask Chase. 'And what's our plan?'

Chase sits on a fat chair. A few rusty springs poke from its bottom.

'Barge's just down the road.' He waves a hand as if Paris is nothing bigger than a village. 'But we'll stay here, out of sight, for a night or two. And the plan is that I have no plan. Good, eh? It's always easier just to make it up as we go along.'

Oh, I think not! And as I'm about to address this issue, Amy runs to the door, wagging her tail. Someone lightly knocks.

'It iz only Vivienne,' a soft voice says. 'I 'ave zoup and cloze.'

Chase heads over, peers through the keyhole, and then lets in our little hostess. She puts a loaded tray onto the table and takes off a red velvet bag slung over her shoulder.

'You are 'iding from bad people,' she says. 'Like I once did. So Vivienne will be like a snappy watchdog

and keep you zafe.' Then she is gone, and the old room closes itself around us as completely as an egg.

'Bedtime,' says Isobel, as we finish our soup and bread. 'And in the morning, we will go exploring!'

Chase up-ends the red bag. Clothes, both black and wildly coloured, spill across the floor.

'It appears we're going to be artists, Georgie-boy.' Chase throws me a purple beret and matching smock. 'And since all Paris loves an artist, we can go wherever we like!'

'I'm not an artist, for one thing,' I tell Chase. 'And secondly, the idea of a smock, a shirt worn backwards, is not only childish but would be quite a handicap if one has to visit the, er, lavatory, in a hurry. I'm sure you can see how the buttons would throw up a whole world of complications and waste precious seconds in an emergency situation.'

'Well, you're going to have to deal with it, Georgie.' Chase hands me the smock and beret, along with a long white cigarette holder and a pair of tall black leather boots. 'Because now that you're an artist, you're going to have to act like one, toilet dramas or not. So it's time to get *jiggy* with it.'

'I shall do my best,' I fire back. 'Without any jigging whatsoever.'

Later, in bed, I look out at the night sky. Paris is a city of wars and rebellions, painters and poets, rascals and rebels, an old city where palaces were built next to people living in poverty. And here we are, caught in an international web woven from millions of dollars that hardly has anything to do with us. I'd prefer to just get on with my life and do things to help the planet and other people. But that's not about to happen – well, not yet.

So I sleep, wondering what tomorrow will bring.

CHAPTER THIRTY-TWO

The next morning, we have breakfast in a sunny room overlooking a tiny courtyard. I'm dressed in long black boots, purple riding pants, and a flouncy white shirt. Thankfully, I swapped the smock for a tight black jacket with gold buttons, and kept the beret and cigarette holder. Chase has on red velvet pants, pointy brown pixie boots, a lime-green shirt, a yellow waistcoat, and a black felt hat with a long red feather in it.

'We look *magnificent*,' he says, as we eat Vivienne's pancakes. 'And you, Isobel, look like a wild princess from a wild country.'

Isobel wears a long black dress embroidered with gold roses, a tight purple jacket with sapphire-blue buttons, ancient tennis shoes, and a gold, red, and black scarf woven through her hair. Even Amy has a tiny green jacket with a silver collar.

'Zis iz 'ow the 'ole world should be!' Vivienne clasps her hands. 'A place where everyone iz free, colourful, and gay! No one will recognise you, Chaze-Gheorge-Izobelle-Amee, but they will think you are famouz! Anyway, 'ave more coffee.'

I consider pointing out to Vivienne that we actually have one name each, but why bother? I do, however, think that perhaps Amy in particular should stop at one coffee, as I'm not sure caffeine is canine-appropriate.

'*Merci*, Vivienne,' I say. 'But I think we've all had enough coffee to—' I was going to say *to last us three days*, but I never get the chance.

The little old lady springs forward and fills up my rather large mug to the very top with thick black liquid.

'Now, Chaze-Gheorge-Izobelle-Amee, you will 'ave energy to chaze all ze bad Germans from Paris, zen 'ide in ze dark forezt before ze Mezzerschmidt aeroplane drop bombz on your 'eads!'

I'd also like to suggest to Vivienne that the Germans in France today are peace-loving tourists on holiday, and that the Second World War ended about eighty years ago, but she's busy shovelling sugar into my mug.

'I 'ear in ze bread zhop zis morning,' she whispers, 'zat zere are Ruzzian tough ladeez looking for runaway thievez from overzeaz. Thiz iz not you, iz it? Per-raps?'

Hmmm! That is an utter fabrication that certainly does sound like something Olga and Katerina *would* come up with. I mean, it's one thing to want to kidnap us, but it's another to accuse us of stealing and muddy our names from one end of Europe to the other, starting in a bread shop in Paris!

'We are *not* thieves,' I inform Vivienne. 'We are the innocent targets of an international kidnapping ring, to be held for ransom for an amount of money that has been lost, but not lost by us.'

Vivienne looks thoughtful, her bright-eyed sparrow's face tight with concern.

'Zomeone muzt owe zomeone a *lot* of money,' she says. 'For zis to 'appen.'

'That,' I say, 'is very true, madame. Unfortunately. For us.'

Our hostess turns away into her miniature kitchen, and comes out with a big tin worn silver with handling and age. With a spoon, she prizes the lid off.

'I can give you French francs,' she says. 'I 'ave five million for a rainy day.'

Chase, Isobel, and I wave Vivienne's money away.

'No, Vivienne,' Isobel reassures her. 'We will look after ourselves. Please keep your money. We just have to get home and everything will work out. But thank you.'

Vivienne slowly stuffs the old notes back into the tin.

'Zeze naughty Germans are like elephantz, no? They nevair forget!'

I think perhaps that the Germans might have forgiven and forgotten more than Vivienne herself, but I doubt that would be a helpful thing to say.

'No, it's not the Germans after us,' I explain. 'It's just some rather unkind folk who have a bee in their bonnet about this money that is missing.'

'You 'ave trouble wiz beez as well as money?' Vivienne raises eyebrows that look like they are drawn on with a biro. 'Iz it a liddle amount of beez and money, or a big amount of beez and money?'

'In the middle somewhere.' Chase finishes his coffee and stands. 'But we do have to avoid these people. And the bees, too, of course. It's most important.'

Vivienne nods. 'I will keep watch. Zoze Germans are probably dizguizing zemzelvez az Mongolianz wiz empty Mongolian bee 'ives! But zey didn't

fool Vivienne in ze bad old dayz and zey will not fool Vivienne in ze year 1999!'

1999? I decide to let that pass and finish my coffee, wishing I hadn't mentioned bees and hoping that the coffee is decaffeinated, although I do feel a bit jumpy – well, a lot jumpy, but if I have a little more energy than normal, it can only be helpful in what are exceptional circumstances.

Chase puts on his pointy hat. 'Let's walk to the river, guys. Relax for a little while.'

Without warning my hand shoots up. '*Grrrrreat* idea, Chase! Yep! Relax! Relax! *Relax!*'

Chase laughs. 'Uh-oh, Izzy,' he says. 'Looks like we've created a caffeine-fired monster again.'

Isobel moves the coffee pot out of my reach. 'George,' she says, 'this coffee-drinking has to stop this very instant.'

'I totally agree,' I say, and jump up. '*NOT!*'

CHAPTER THIRTY-THREE

It is a cold blue-sky morning as we walk down to the Seine — well, Isobel, Chase, and Amy walk, but I hop, skip, and jump while waving my cigarette holder that now has a blue plastic flower poked into the end.

'Nothing like a cup of the old coffee to get you going,' I say, and leap-frog a post box taller than I am. 'Boy, I sure feel *springy*!'

Chase puts a hand on my shoulder. 'Georgie, calm down. The traffic drives on the other side of the road here. You don't want to go under a speeding bicycle.'

'Good point.' I take a slow, steadying breath in through my nose. 'Can you smell coffee, Chase?' I swivel around. 'Look. There's a cafe. And another and another—'

'George,' Isobel says, 'there are a million cafes in Paris. You can't have coffee in every one. Let's just go down the steps to the river and watch these people painting. We might pick up some ideas on how real artists act.'

'That's a *good* point, Isobel, and a *great* idea!'

'No need to shout, George.' Chase laughs. 'Boy, you're on fire this morning!'

We walk down to the wide brown river. I see the huge Notre Dame cathedral that rises from an island; I see a stone bridge, and large black barges tied to thick steel rings. And standing behind four wooden artist's easels are four artists painting this rather elegant scene. We sit quietly to watch and enjoy.

The painters, I see, are interpreting the scene differently. Now, I don't know much about art but I do know what I like – gumtrees, a vase of flowers, perhaps an antique coffee pot or new coffee pot, I'm not fussy. Perhaps even just a coffee *sack* would suit me the way I feel this morning!

'This school of painting,' I explain, perhaps a little too loudly, 'is known as *plein air*, Chase and Isobel. Amy, too, if you're listening. Meaning it is done *outside*, in the open air, with the artist trying to capture the real world, although you can see this short dumpy chap on the left is struggling a bit—'

The painter, a little man with a floppy black moustache, a green smock and matching beret, turns around.

'*Shhh!* You know nothing! You can do better? Okay! It's your turn!' With that, he rips his painting off the easel, balls it up, and throws it in the river. 'Here.' He comes up to me, holding out his brush like a dagger and his paint palette like a shield. 'I triple dare you, Mr Purple Britches! You are a nasty critic with no talent but much rudeness and stupid hair!'

'Well, sir,' I say, feeling the full effects of the coffee, 'since you put it like that, how can I refuse?' So I take the brush and palette and advance towards the sheet of white paper on the easel. 'Pointillist?' I ask, utilising my coffee-fuelled recall of every art gallery tour my mother ever took me on, which would be upwards of fifty, I'd guess. 'Impressionist? Romanticist? Realist? Cubist? Fauvist?' I attack the paper as if I am at bayonet practice with the Tapley Grammar Cadets. 'Or all of the above? Which will be now known as the George Parker school of coffee-fuelled, sugar-coated, pancake-produced creativity!'

The little artist stands with his hands on his hips. 'You are a fool with bad trousers and smoking plastic flowers!'

The coffee has located my long-lost artistic abilities that have remained buried at Tapley Grammar, because artistic boys are ordered to voluntarily leave the school or endlessly repeat Year Five, even if they are one hundred and ninety centimetres tall and weigh ninety kilograms.

'Touché!' I slash diagonally with red paint. 'A daring dash of *romanticism* here!' I dab some smudgy blue here, there, and everywhere. 'A splodge of *impressionism* there!' Now I jab black dots like an industrial sewing machine gone mad. 'And a spot of *pointillism* here! Plus plenty of George *Parkerisms* everywhere else!'

A painted river appears, as does a cathedral, a barge, a bridge, and *voilà*! Paris is captured in a miraculous bubble of brilliance, but I don't hang around, as the little artist chap seems like he might want to chuck me in the water.

'Thank you and goodnight!' I back away bowing, waving my beret like a flyswat, and my cigarette holder like a magic wand. 'Remember, art is the answer! Even if I don't know the question!'

Chase and Isobel catch me up as I head off along the river. 'That was incredible, Georgie,' Chase says. 'You're a genius.'

'Oh, it was nothing,' I say. 'Nothing I could ever do again, I mean. I don't know what came over me.'

'*Coffee* came over you,' Isobel says. 'You have to

be careful you don't overdose, George. Anything could happen. Your entire system is obviously hyper-sensitive to caffeine.'

I laugh loudly from where I've swung up into the branches of a tree.

'And is that a *bad* thing, Isobel?'

We sit beside the slow-flowing Seine and watch Paris and its people go about their daily lives. Chase writes a postcard to Clemmy, informing her of where we are, and Amy is trying to make friends with a poodle, which isn't going very well, given the language barrier. I ask Isobel how she's feeling.

'I can't remember everything,' she says, her pale face surrounded by her wild black hair. 'But I can remember our house, my school, the smell of the garden, and the view from my bedroom. Are you homesick, George?'

As I'm not sure whether my *home* is my house, where I don't live, or Tapley Grammar, where I do live, it's a hard question.

'I'd like to get back to study,' I answer. 'Tapley needs help in the science and maths areas, as all the best students spend their time looking for lost cricket balls or campaigning to have whaling brought back as a school sport. Eventually, I want to help children in other places. Like the Congo, just to pull a country out of the hat.'

'Very good, George.' Isobel sips a cup of tea. 'That's beautiful thinking.'

CHAPTER THIRTY-FOUR

We hop on and off buses to confuse anyone who's following us, and one hour later, we are standing under the Eiffel Tower – a tower that I'm familiar with, as I have a scale model at Tapley made from eighty thousand burnt matches. It was built by my Uncle Graham, who lives in a caravan with his executive personal assistant, an albino guinea pig named Simon (although I would suggest that Simon is really more just a pet).

'*Mon Dieu*,' says Chase, looking up through the lattice of girders that appear to soar upwards forever. 'I don't know why they call it the *Awful* Tower, George. It looks all right to me.'

I would classify that remark as *incredibly* culturally insensitive.

'If that's your idea of a joke, Chase,' I mutter, 'I'm not sure our French friends would find it very funny. And if the relatives of Gustave Eiffel, the designer, happened to be picnicking in the area – and that's not out of the question – imagine how they'd feel?'

Chase laughs. 'How did I ever get on at school without you, George?'

'Let's find the stairs and go up,' says Isobel, holding Amy. 'It'll be fun.'

So, on a magnificent steel staircase dappled by sunshine and shadows, we set off upwards.

'Hey, Georgie,' says Chase, after about ten minutes of climbing, 'this Eiffel Tower's certainly giving us an *eyeful* of Paris now. Look how high we are. Imagine if *I fell* off?'

Right! I am *determined* to put an end to these insensitive comments about this elegant monument.

'Chase,' I say, choosing my words with great care, 'regarding the Eiffel Tower, I've had *my fill*—' No, that's not going to work. 'I *feel*—' Darn, I did it again. 'I've had more than *enough* of your *awful* Eiffel—' Oh, I give up.

We arrive at an observation deck far above the ground. Below, Paris spreads in all directions like a pale-coloured tapestry. Usually I'm terrified of heights, but the caffeine in my system has diminished my nervousness to a point where I feel quite fine.

'Ever thought you could fly, Chase?' I imagine gliding over to England, perhaps popping into a tearoom and stirring things up by ordering a pot of coffee. 'Sometimes it really does seem possible.'

Chase grabs my arm. 'You're under the influence of sugar and caffeine, Georgie-boy. A cup of coffee can't defy gravity, and neither can you.'

I shake his hand off. 'I *know* that! This is all to do with the imagination and nothing to do with coffee. Although if there's a cup going, I wouldn't say no.' I look around. 'Surely there must be a machine or something? What's wrong with these people?'

'You've had too much already,' says Isobel. 'And don't give me any more of that *not* business. Because I am *not* listening.'

I don't reply, as my razor-sharp senses have detected some extremely suspicious-looking characters arriving on our deck.

'The enemy,' I hiss, 'is here!'

It's *Roland*, wearing yellow pants, a lavender shirt and pink jacket, with a handgun in a shoulder holster! Beside him, in blue overalls and carrying mops, are Katerina and Olga, followed by some musicians with bongos and an accordion, which is confusing.

My mind is racing; Olga has the lift covered, Katerina the stairs, and Roland is coming my way.

'Chase,' I whisper, 'I'll get their attention while you take Isobel and Amy down the tower. We'll meet in the Eiffel Trifle, Coffee and Truffle cafe across the road. Order me a double-shot short long black.' I have a sudden thought. 'No, make it a triple. See you soon.'

Chase pokes me hard in the chest. 'You're supposed to be smart, George. Don't do anything stupid.'

'Don't worry,' I say. 'I was xylophone class safety monitor for five years. In all that time, no one ever forgot their ear plugs, suffered concussion, or developed a repetitive strain injury. Now *go!*'

An accordion begins to play a swirling gypsy melody that interfaces with the creative centre of my coffee-sensitised brain, sending me twirling like a talented tornado to leap up onto the rail. The crowd is amazed! And so am I, just quietly.

'Ooh-lah-lah!'

Oh my goodness, I think, looking down. But this is Georgie-boy's time to shine!

I do a dazzling coffee-fuelled run along a girder. And when the music abruptly stops, so do I – luckily, as there's nowhere else to go but down.

'Grab zat monkey-boy!' Roland yells. ''Iz danzing iz diszrezpecting French pipple! I am polizeman drezzed in paztel colourz and 'ee iz awful Oztralian, pozzibly Ned Kellee, who zteal zheep and pud 'im in a tuckair bag bezide billybonk!'

I swing up onto another girder. 'That's racism, Roland!' I yell. 'Besides, you're not a policeman but a mediocre magician. And I would never be unkind to sheep. In fact, I favour wool over *any* synthetic fibre you can name! I would also consider vegetarianism, but unfortunately it's outlawed at my school!'

The music starts, and this time it's a traditional Jewish folk song called 'Hava Nagila', which starts slowly then gets faster. And as the crowd claps, I make a charge towards the lift. But Roland blocks my exit, shouting.

'Ziz Gheorge-rat muzt be arrezted! Ze tuckair bag 'az no air holes. Ze sheeps, 'ee 'az nightmarez about zis!'

'*Let us sing,*' I sing. '*Let us rejoice! With a happy heart!*' Which is truly how I feel, because Isobel and Chase have snuck away, and now I can make my dash for freedom. Well, I could've, until I see that Amy has come back to look for me!

Actually, no. She's chasing a huge black rat that sends people running in all directions, which fortunately results in the crowd pinning Roland into a corner and pushing Olga and Katerina back into the lift – leaving me free to grab Amy, who has seized the rat, and down the stairs we go!

I leave the rat safe and sound in the souvenir shop, blend into the passing parade of people, and then make my way into rather dimly lit Eiffel Trifle, Coffee and Truffle cafe on the boulevard.

'Pssst! Over here, George!'

In a dark corner, under old coach lamps, I see Isobel and Chase. This cafe is a wonderful little place, made of ancient black timber, with a sprinkling of rather *varied* customers.

'Whew-ee.' I collapse onto the worn leather seat. 'I can't believe I did that. I normally hate heights.' When I was small, instead of a treehouse, I had a house-tree, which was a little cubby on the ground built around a tree that had been disinfected and cling-wrapped. 'So,' I say. 'What d'you think the coffee's like here?'

'You don't need any more coffee,' Isobel says firmly.

I feel a little disappointed. 'Perhaps I could have one of those green drinks, then? That all these other people are having? I'd say they'd be a pea or bean-based beverage, Isobel. Very healthful.'

Again, Isobel heads me off. 'No, George,' she whispers. 'They're drinking absinthe. It's a potent kind of a drug. Or it used to be, in France in the old days.'

Well, I certainly *won't* be having that because, along with polyester pants and plastic supermarket bags, Parkers do not do drugs!

Chase looks around. 'We're safe in here,' he says. 'Because of how we look. This is an artists' cafe. You know, writers, painters, poets, all those nutty sorts of people. No tourists.'

From a rear door, I see a large lady in a green dress and black jacket bring in a tray loaded with bowls and bread. She comes to our table and puts the tray down.

'*Bon appétit*,' she murmurs, her dark eyes flashing, her gold earrings swinging. 'Welcome to you, the artists.'

'*Merci, madame.*' Isobel holds out a twenty euro note, which the lady waves away. '*Non, merci, madame.* Your necklace.' She points to one of the glass necklaces that Isobel made in hospital in New York. 'Trade.'

The necklace is made of big chunks of old ginger-coloured glass joined with some kind of silver chain. Isobel gives it to the lady, who puts it in a pocket then rubs Isobel's pale hands in her own, which are weighed down by rings with red and green stones.

'Now, as well as beautiful soup, you have good luck.' The lady looks at Isobel intently. 'Where are you sleeping tonight?'

'L'Hotel Geranium,' Isobel replies.

The lady nods. 'Ah, good. I organise you safely home in a few minutes.'

'Great,' Chase says. 'Thank you, madame.'

The lady walks away, we begin on our meal, and the noise in the cafe rises.

'This is what the *real* Paris used to be like,' Chase says. 'Full of artists, actors, writers, ghosts, and mystery. Like, check *this* cat out.'

A wild-looking young man comes into the cafe. He holds a three-cornered hat, his black hair curls to his shoulders, and he has on a long leather coat and tall boots. He strides to our table.

'I take you to L'Hotel Geranium,' he says. 'Luludja, the Romani queen, has ordered it.'

The lady in green nods from behind the bar.

'*Oui*,' Luludja says. 'Go with Tommy. He can be trusted.'

Isobel shrugs. 'It's probably safer leaving with someone these people know than getting on the bus or train. Roland will be sure to be watching the underground stations and stops around here.'

'Good enough for me,' says Chase, so we quietly make our exit.

Outside, a thick fog swirls slowly through the night-dark trees. The Eiffel Tower is a haunting four-legged presence disappearing into an unseen sky. Standing in deep shadow, I see four black horses and a black carriage with golden lamps.

'Far out!' Chase claps. 'That is *so* cool! Let's go.'

So we climb into the coach. There is a sound of jangling and iron horseshoes striking hard stone, and we are off into the cold, misty, and mysterious Parisian evening. And although there are no safety belts fitted or a colourful brochure to pass the time, we make it safely back to L'Hotel Geranium on

Tommy's tourist coach via the romantic backstreets of the City of Light that is currently quite dark. Then we watch the rattling black coach and black horses disappear into the fog and silence returns.

'Now, George,' says Chase. 'Do you think that would've happened if we'd stayed home?'

CHAPTER THIRTY-FIVE

The next morning, I wake to see Isobel sitting on one of the old striped chairs. Sun is streaming through the windows and the wooden floor shines like gold.

'Time to get up, George,' she says. 'I think we should go to the barge. We've put Vivienne through enough. Why don't you head down the hall to the bathroom, then we'll get going.'

And there I am, wallowing in the bath like a happy dugong off Hayman Island, when three shadows pass by the frosted-glass skylight. Suddenly I am a happy dugong no more. I hop out of the bath, grab my towel and race back towards our room. Then I give the secret door-knock code, which I now feel is perhaps a little drawn-out for such an emergency.

Bang, bang, bang, bang, bang, bang, bang, bang, bang, bang, bang, bang, bang, bang, bang, BANG!

Chase opens the door and I dive inside.

'Guys! And Amy! We gotta go right now!' I don't even worry about running the words *got* and *to* together. 'Roland's on the roof. Just grab everything and let's fly. We gotta go NOW!'

In two minutes, I am dressed in my own old clothes, we're out the door, and standing in the hotel's reception.

'I've already paid the bill,' Isobel says. 'Where will we go?'

'If Roland's on the roof,' Chase says, 'we'll head down to the river. One, two, three! Run!'

Then we're outside, running down the sunny street. From the roof, I hear shouting.

'Zere iz zat dirty razkal, Gheorge! And zhoze other Oztralian criminalz who zteal money and pozzibly zheep, as I zaid yezterday! Queeck! Exztend ze laddair, ladeez!'

I turn to see Roland, Olga, and Katerina, all dressed in black, lowering a ladder from the roof.

'Grab a bike, George!' Chase points to a rack of grey rental bikes. 'Come on!'

'Sorry to be a party pooper, Chase,' I say, not moving. 'No can do. For us to ride legally, they have to be paid for. But even more importantly, we have no helmets.'

Isobel pokes money into the slots. 'All clear!' She takes a bike from the rack. 'It's okay, George. Today is National No-Bike-Helmet Day. So get a move on!'

Well, that's a stroke of luck! So with a clear conscience, I grab a bike, and we wobble away downhill towards the river. I can hear Roland shouting.

'Queek, liddle flower Olga and 'appy piglet Katerina! Ze razcalz 'ave bicyclez!'

I glance behind us and see Olga and Katerina are sprinting like relay runners who couldn't care less about the baton change.

'Pedals to the metal!' I yell. 'Accelerate, in other words!'

I realise that although I thought I couldn't ride a bike, it seems that I can. I also make a mental note to write to the French government regarding the dangers of National No-Bike-Helmet Day, but that can wait. Instead, I follow Chase and Isobel.

'This way!' Chase turns onto the river path. 'Down the ramp, George!'

'Okay,' I say, but what I hoped was a ramp turns out to be steps – and down I go in a teeth-chattering, bone-battering, bottom-bouncing, death-defying descent that somehow nevertheless ends with me remaining upright, and then we're off again,

Roland's Russian relay team a hundred metres behind us.

'There!' Chase skids to a halt and points. 'That ferry! It's going. Let's catch it!'

Ahead of us is a large white tourist boat. So we ride like mad, hide our bikes behind a tree, and run up the gangplank as the last ropes are being thrown off. Yes! We're safe, because the gap between our ferry and the shore is now at least ten metres. I take a deep breath and look around.

'Oh, good show,' I say. 'They sell coffee!'

CHAPTER THIRTY-SIX

Since it's such a sunny morning, we sit on the top deck and watch the beautiful stone city of Paris slowly reveal itself. Having almost recovered from the shock of riding without a helmet, I realise I'm thirsty.

'I'll just pop down to the onboard cafe,' I say, 'and buy us all a drink. I'm a little dehydrated. Cycling, although healthful, can be harmful if one doesn't re-fill one's tank, so to speak.'

Isobel nods. 'That's very nice of you, George. But no coffee, as your judgement seems to seriously suffer.'

Chase laughs. 'That's when he's at his best, Izzy. When he's out of control.'

I don't think I'm *ever* out of control! It's just that in certain challenging *situations*, I have to act accordingly.

'No coffee,' I inform Isobel. 'I promise.'

Isobel smiles, relaxes, and takes Amy out of my backpack. So I venture downstairs and buy Isobel an orange juice, Chase a hot chocolate, and, to celebrate my bicycling skills, I purchase something called a Red Bull on a three-for-one deal.

'*Merci, monsieur*,' I say, and drink the first two Red Bulls right there, where I can easily recycle the containers. 'Mmmmm, what a lovely caffeine-free morning!'

With a clear conscience, I take the drinks upstairs, and enjoy my third Red Bull as we pass through a city that is more than a thousand years old.

'*What* are you *doing*, George?' Isobel looks shocked. 'Red Bulls contain caffeine! They're high-energy drinks.'

I finish my third in one gulp and crush it. 'Are they? Well, nobody told me.' I throw the can into a bin twenty metres away. 'What a *shot!*' I jump up. 'Yes *sir*, it's the George Parker *big* show! Ka boom! Kapow! Georgie's really *feelin'* it now! Say what, Isobel?' I sit down, stand up, then sit down again. 'I had to replace energy lost riding the bicycle,' I explain. 'I actually feel *quite* exhausted.'

No I don't, I feel GREAT!

That is, until I notice that the ferry is doing a slow U-turn, and we are heading back exactly in the direction we came from!

'Uh-oh,' I say. 'It might be swim-time quite shortly, folks. Not to worry,' I add. 'The water looks a rather pleasant shade of brown and I'm somewhat of a freshwater side-stroke specialist.'

'Side-stroke went out of fashion with woollen bathers,' Chase says. 'A hundred years ago.'

'Absolutely *incorrect*, Chase.' I raise my finger to address that point. 'I am still rocking – although not today – a home-knitted pair of dark green woollen bathers with a red and beige elastic belt.' Just thinking about them takes me back to days spent splashing about in a rock pool fifty metres above the high-tide mark, for safety's sake. 'Quick-drying, too. Just a day or two on the line and they're ready for any aquatic activity you can think of, including shell-gathering, supervised shallow-immersion paddling, or the complex but utterly fascinating pastime of classifying east coast Australian seaweeds.'

Chase laughs, although I'm not sure why, because Roland and the Russians are waiting on the dock. And I doubt they're too interested in taking a river cruise or discussing the many positives of woollen bathers.

Code red!

We can't escape by swimming or jumping onto a passing bridge. For a moment, I consider chatting to the captain in such a lively fashion that he forgets to stop at the dock, but he's wearing headphones and drumming on the dashboard with pencils, so that seems impractical.

'They've got all exits covered,' Chase says. 'We're cornered.'

'We're not cornered,' I say. 'We're *inconvenienced*!' My mind is racing. 'Chase, Isobel, Amy, hide on board until I give you a signal from the pathway. Then leave the boat fast!'

Isobel looks worried. 'How will you get to the path, George?'

'I'm going to bamboozle Roland,' I say, 'with linguistic acrobatics, clothing confabulation, and show-stopping physical obfuscation. That will in turn completely flummox Olga, confuse Katerina, and out-fox the lot of them. Then we'll be free to disembark and bicycle to freedom!'

Yes, sometimes the simplest plans are the best.

I tuck my singlet and shirt into my pants and tuck my pants into my socks for a rather smart and aerodynamic look.

'Count me down!' I nod at Chase. 'In any language you like because it's a *Red Bull* kind of a morning!'

Chase holds up three fingers. 'Three, two—'

'Sorry, can't wait!' I *dance* through the crowd and stop at the top of the gangway. 'Attention, ladies and gentlemen!' Everybody looks. 'George Parker – that's me – will now attempt a triple somersault ferry boat dismount with the idea of fooling that rotten-ratbag-masquerading-as-a-magician Roland, who waits for me at the bottom of the gangway. Stand back, folks! And don't try this at home!'

Oh, man, this will be *too* funny.

'You are trepped, ztupit Gheórge!' Roland laughs. 'No more tuckair-begging sheepz by boiling 'im in billabonk! It iz game ovair and out!'

I skip down the gangplank then back up the gangplank, before disappearing into the ferry with Roland in hot pursuit. Quickly, I duck into a toilet, reverse my autumn-leaf-coloured polar fleece bush-walking top, tie on three life jackets, wet my Mohawk down, take off my glasses, pull on my now-high-visibility-orange bushwalking top, and saunter out like a balding passenger who's eaten a few too many chocolate croissants.

'Scuse me, pal,' I say to Roland, 'I think I'll just mosey on into town and buy me some real Paris-style Texan flapjacks. Which way is France?'

Roland barely looks at me. 'No flapjackz in Pariz, Mizter Zan Fat-frizco.' He points to the riverbank. 'All zat place iz France, you zero intelligenze tourizt.'

'Thank you kindly, sir.' I wander down the gangway, wave to Chase and Isobel, then stroll off to where we've hidden the bikes. Oh, *too* easy!

Woof, woof, woof!

Except that I see Amy running down the gang-plank, winding her way between people's legs to jump joyously into my arms. And now I see Roland and he is moving fast.

'Katerina ant Olga!' Roland points. 'Zat fat idiot wiz zee liddle zpotted pippy-dock is stupit Gheorge! Go, ladeeze, go!'

'To the bikes!' We start to run. 'To the bikes!'

Unfortunately, there is one bike missing.

'Hop onto this one with me, Isobel,' I say. 'I'll provide the power. You navigate.'

'We'll go to the barge, George.' Isobel gets set. 'It's down the river. The way we came.'

I start to pedal.

'Roland's got a bike,' Chase yells. 'All three of them are on it!'

Of course! Olga and Katerina are *acrobats* – they could do this stuff all day long!

'Normally,' I shout to Chase, 'there's no shame in coming second or even twenty-second – although one hundred and twenty-second wouldn't be great, I admit. But today, this is one race we *cannot* afford to lose! *Go!*'

I glance over my shoulder and see Olga on one side of the bike, Katerina counter-balancing on the other, and Roland pedalling.

Isobel shouts. 'Look out, George! A dog!'

I swerve around the dog, then swerve along the river, then swerve around a lady, then swerve around a rubbish bin then—

'George,' Isobel says, 'we've stopped.'

Oh, so we have. And here comes Roland.

'You are a zickly zyclizt, Gheorge!' Roland strains at the pedals. 'Whereaz I am a zupreme shampion. 'Old on, liddle ladeeze, we go like pointy-nozzed Concorde jet!'

I pedal hard, even though I have a terrible stitch in my side.

'Pain is simply weakness leaving the body,' I tell Isobel. 'I'm like Superman!'

'Left across the next bridge, George.' Isobel points. 'Then we hide, because the barge is tied up right there.'

I see hundreds of boats in a rectangular mooring basin just off the main river.

'Perfect!'

I cross the bridge, plunge down a ramp, and ride kamikaze-style straight into a mass of shrubbery.

Ka-shoosh!

Chase follows, bringing autumn early as we crouch as quietly as we can and watch Roland, Olga, and Katerina ride right past us.

Brilliant!

We hide for an hour, return our bikes to another rental stand, then pick up the key to the barge from the office of the Bassin de l'Arsenal, which is basically just a big basin where boats are kept. Walking down the quay, I imagine that the barge will be old, rusty, and ratty, but the *Solange* is like a long, narrow, beautiful house

226

with polished copper portholes, chrome handrails, and shining wooden decks. We go aboard and into the saloon.

'This is a dreamboat,' I say, looking at the paintings, the expensive furniture, and an elegant galley complete with a rather complicated-looking silver coffee machine.

'I'll just fire up the old coffee thing, guys,' I add casually. 'I sure could do with a cup.'

'Oh, no you won't,' Isobel says. 'We're all going to rest. And go to bed early. This is our chance to plan our next move.'

'I'll text Clemmy,' Chase says. 'You never know where or when she might pop up.'

So we sit and look out at the beautiful city of Paris, and I know I will never be the same simple George Parker again.

'Boy, Isobel,' I say, staring at a peculiar painting of a lady – well, I think it's a lady, with a wonky eye and an incomplete jigsaw-type of body – 'that's a very interesting artwork you have there.'

'It's a Picasso,' Izzy says. 'An original.'

Good golly! It could be worth tens of millions!

'We'll take it with us when we leave,' Chase says. 'It might come in handy.'

Isobel folds her feet up under herself on the couch.

'You know, George,' she says, 'all this running and hiding makes me wonder if perhaps our family does do bad things.'

'That's true, Isobel,' I agree. 'But the people investing in your dad's investment fund must know they might make a lot of money or lose a lot.'

Chase nods. 'And this time they lost it. Bad luck.'

'And bad luck for us.' Then Isobel smiles. 'But it was such good luck that you boys got me out of that hospital.'

'Yep, and it was a lot of fun.' Chase looks at his phone. 'Clemmy's in London shooting a commercial for Jet Ranger helicopters. She certainly gets around.'

She certainly does.

Amy and I have our own beautiful cabin with two portholes. I am so tired that I barely have the strength to even up my shoelaces, do my finger exercises for quick calculator use, and clean and floss my teeth before sliding under a doona so thick, light, and fluffy that it's like a warm cloud. Then I sleep and sleep and sleep.

CHAPTER THIRTY-SEVEN

We spend the next day on the barge keeping out of sight, checking what's going on outside, and occasionally watching the wide-screen television, although only Isobel can understand what's being said.

'Look!' She points. 'It's Mum and Dad on the French news! Shhh! I've got to hear what they're saying.'

We watch in strained silence, Isobel listening intently to the French newsreader as pictures of the Landon-Bonds boarding a luxury yacht in Monte Carlo flash across the screen. Then they're gone, replaced by a story that seems to be about an English pig that has had twenty-seven piglets, which is evidently a world record.

'So what did they say, Izzy?' Chase's normally sunny face is tight and tense. Even his eyes have changed to a deeper, dark grey. 'Good news or bad news? I mean about our parents, not the pig.'

Isobel expels a long breath. 'Well, basically, they said that our folks have applied to become citizens of

Monaco, but the government wouldn't accept them, due to some shady worldwide financial dealings they're *allegedly* involved in. So they had to leave.'

'To go where?' Chase looks upset, and I don't blame him; it's not a very nice thing, I would imagine, for your parents to try changing countries without even bothering to tell you. My parents have a policy of informing me when they're moving from one room to another in case of fire, flood, roof cave-ins, or an earthquake cutting the house in half. 'Didn't they say?'

Isobel shakes her head. 'No, all that was said was that Mr and Mrs Landon-Bond were setting sail for destinations unknown.'

Chase puts his bare feet up on the coffee table and rests his chin on his hand.

'Oh, well.' He looks out at white apartment buildings that rise over the mooring basin. 'Why don't I just give Dad a ring and find out *what* his plans are?'

Isobel, now wearing her own clothes, looks fresh and cool, and a little bit older.

'Good idea. Because if we truly are criminals or belong to a criminal family, I want to know.'

Chase takes a deep breath. 'Oh, let's go and get

something to eat instead. I'll ring later. An hour or two won't make any difference.'

So, under the cover of darkness, we slip out into another mysterious Parisian night where clouds gather to roam a wide black sky lit by a ghostly moon. And then, after some French fries and crepes, we slip back to our wonderful barge, the *Solange*, and sleep.

CHAPTER THIRTY-EIGHT

We wake to a cold, clear day, with mist slow-dancing over the boats resting at their moorings.

'I'll check out the coffee machine,' I volunteer generously as we eat toast and jam at the kitchen table. 'I can figure it out, I think. Besides, it's safer to stay on board than go out to a cafe.'

Isobel looks at me sternly. 'Maybe later, George. Because coffee at breakfast might speed you up a little too much a little too early.'

I don't necessarily agree with that: coffee doesn't *speed* me up, it simply *refreshes* me.

'I couldn't get through to the folks,' Chase informs us. 'I guess they're out of range. So, Izzy, what's on this morning's agenda?'

'We could go out for coffee,' I suggest hopefully, 'if we're careful.'

'You've already tried that angle, George.' Isobel shoots me a look. 'Perhaps you and Amy can stay on board and keep lookout while Chase and I buy supplies.' She then pinches a fold of my Tapley Chargers T-shirt that features an eight-hundred-word written report on the 2014 World Chess Championship between Magnus Carlson and Viswanathan Anand. 'I might even pick you up a new shirt or two.'

I steal a look at the coffee machine, sitting there like a spaceship ready for take-off.

'That's very nice of you, Isobel,' I say. 'Amy and I will stand guard. You can *rely* on us.'

Isobel holds up a hand. 'George, be good, okay? Not a *single* coffee. I'll bring you a small one back, if you like.'

'Yes, that would be lovely, Isobel.' I sit on one of the couches, knuckles on my knees and a trustworthy smile on my face. 'One small coffee would be *just* the ticket!'

Chase and Isobel leave the barge and I sit looking out over the wide and misty river. Then I take a peek at the coffee machine.

'Why not learn something new?' I ask Amy. 'And if that happens to be how to work a coffee machine, then so be it.'

It appears that Amy has no objections, so I turn the machine on. Stage One complete!

The temperature gauge on the coffee machine hits ninety-two degrees Celsius, which, according to the handbook, is ideal.

'Water *ready*!' I inform Amy, who watches me hard at work. 'Coffee *located,* access *obtained*.' I snip the corner off a large packet of ground coffee then tamp a decent shot into the silver thing that fits perfectly into the machine. 'Time to steam the long-life milk.'

I pour milk into the stainless jug, push a button, hear a hiss, turn a black knob, and lo and behold, we're in business – the *coffee* business!

'How about a pupaccino, Amy?' I froth the milk as liquid gold drips steadily into a big white cup. 'Seems a waste to tip beautiful George Parker *barista*-made coffee down the sink. Besides, Isobel said not to have a *single* coffee. Meaning it's fine to have at least a couple.'

One of the many good things about numbers is that they *never* lie.

So, in the pursuit of coffee-making perfection, Amy and I set to work, and an hour later we're still hard at it. And when Chase and Isobel come back on board, I've only got two clean cups left out of twelve.

'Don't worry, Isobel,' I assure her, as she deposits

shopping bags on the table. 'I haven't had a *single* cup. And I'll do the washing up. I might even paint the barge. So. Feel like a brew?' I let the steam fly. 'Today we're offering *genuine* Italian-style cappuccino, frappaccino, long and short macchiato, a magnificent mocha, a George Parker Melbourne-inspired Americano, a fab flat white, or a pupaccino that I don't really recommend, as it comes with a *dog* biscuit!'

Isobel comes over rather quickly. 'Stop it, George! You said you wouldn't have one.'

I make her a latte with a love heart in the cream. Or perhaps it's a turnip.

'I haven't had one,' I say. 'I've had ten. Anyway,' I add sugar to Chase's cup, 'anyone know how to get the music going? Then I might swab the deck because I've got energy to burn. Even better, speaking of burning, I'll build a steel furnace!'

'Sit, George!' Isobel drags me to the couch. 'No more coffee. I'm going to put the supplies away. You stay here until I come back. And don't do anything silly.'

'Okay,' I answer, 'I'll just sit down and mentally cross-reference the major ocean currents with the migration patterns of my six favourite whale species. That's always a fun way to kill half an hour.'

'Yeah, you do that.' Isobel picks up her backpack. 'Just don't drink any more coffee.'

Isobel leaves for the saloon and Chase flops down on the couch. 'Feel like some chocolate, Georgie? I could just nip over to the snack bar and grab some. Izzy wouldn't mind because she wouldn't know.'

'Great idea,' I say. 'And while you're away, I might just pop up into the wheelhouse for a wee look around. Just to get a feel for things.'

'Back soon,' Chase whispers, and heads out onto the sunny deck, bound for the shore.

Amy and I head to the stern of the *Solange*, climb the wooden ladder into the wheelhouse, and inspect the wheel, dials, and buttons.

'Check it out, Amy.' The wheelhouse windows give a clear view of the barge's long timber deck, the wide river, and the sunny banks of the Seine, busy with people. 'And look, one little green button starts the whole thing,' I say. 'And the gear box only has forward, reverse, neutral. It's no Ferrari, that's for sure.'

Amy jumps up on the dashboard and looks outside. This does a couple of things. Firstly, it alerts me to the fact that Chase is sprinting back to the barge like a madman, and secondly, Amy's paw has landed squarely on the green starter button. The *Solange's* massive diesel engine throbs with life!

'Not so sure you should've done that, Amy,' I say. 'Isobel will get mad at you.'

Chase leaps onto the barge and comes up the wheelhouse ladder like a monkey.

'Roland's coming, Georgie!' Chase is puffing and panting, his hands flying about. 'They're searching every boat. There's nowhere to hide!'

'That won't matter,' I say, with more than a little coffee-flavoured courage, 'if we're not here.' My pulse rate accelerates. 'You throw the mooring ropes off and I'll back her out. Amy's already started her up.'

Chase's face goes pale. 'This is a two-hundred-tonne steel barge, George! It's massive. You can't drive it.'

'That's true, Chase,' I say seriously. 'Because you don't drive a barge, you *sail* it!'

Chase lights up. 'It's our *only* chance. Go for it, Geepy. Go for it!'

CHAPTER THIRTY-NINE

From the wheelhouse, I see Chase dragging in the ropes that tie us to the dock. He turns and gives me the thumbs-up.

'Stand by to reverse, Officer Amy.' I clunk the silver lever into R. 'Engine reversed, sir! Revolutions up. Oh, a bit more, kid.' I feel the power lift quite substantially. 'As we're in a hurry.'

Slowly, the *Solange* draws backwards from the dock. Amy, standing on the dashboard, barks excitedly, her paws starting the windscreen wipers, which isn't super-helpful.

'Steady,' I say, switching them off. 'I have to work out the steering.'

Barges don't have brakes, which I've just figured out. Nor do they seem to go in a straight line. But by turning the wheel to the left, or *port*, I somehow manage to have the *Solange* sitting with her black steel bow pointed to the open river. So I select

Forward gear, lift the revs, and just as Amy turns on the sound system, Isobel appears. And it appears she's furious.

'What are you *doing*, George?'

'That's *Captain* George,' I say. 'And you'll have to speak up. This Strauss waltz is rather loud. First Officer Amy just put it on.'

Da da da da dah! Duh-duh! Duh-duh!

Isobel turns off the music, which I was quite enjoying.

'Stop the boat!' Isobel yells. 'Are you *mad*?'

I point to the dock, where Roland, Olga, and Katerina are running after us – hopelessly, it seems, thank goodness, because they all have wetsuits, flippers, knives, and spear guns.

'I had no choice, Izzy.' This is true. 'Although I must say I'm enjoying it.' This is also true. 'Most people, at some point in their lives, Isobel, would like to run away to sea. So I'm killing two birds with one stone, which is a—'

From the dock, I can hear Roland.

'You ztinking Gheorge Parkair boat burglair! I will ketch you zomewhair on zis magnifizent but treacher-rooz waterway zelebrated in zongs and tourizt broshurez! And zen ze reward will be mine and you will be nozzing but an 'orrible memory I will forget az zoon az pozzible.'

You won't catch me, Rolly old chap, I think, as I steer the beautiful black barge downstream towards Normandy. *Unless you're a hell of a good swimmer.*

'Anyway, Isobel,' I continue, 'why don't you go and put the kettle on?'

She slaps my arm. 'If we ever get off this thing alive,' she says. 'You're in big trouble.'

'I'll already be in big trouble,' I say, 'if I end up hitting the Pont de Sully bridge here, which was built in the year—'

'Shut *up*, George!' Isobel turns away. 'I'm going downstairs. And you'd better work out what you're doing and fast!'

I pull a face at First Officer Amy but keep quiet, even though I am the captain. And down the river we peacefully go, until I realise that Roland might get his hands on a boat that might be somewhat – or a lot – faster than ours. I increase the *Solange*'s speed, which suddenly seems very slow. Then, since a monstrous white tourist ferry is coming straight towards us, it seems rather rapid.

'Hold on to your hats, ladies and gents,' I say. 'Hard a-port!'

Amy runs along the instrument panel, barking at the big white boat, and hits the music, the horn, and the heater.

'Well, it's *all* happening now,' I mutter. 'But don't panic, kid. There's no point.'

Chase's smiling face appears in the wheelhouse. He looks rather impressed with what Amy and I are managing to do.

'I have chocolate, Captain.'

'Well done, Officer Chase.' I'm getting the hang of steering the *Solange* now by anticipating the slow swinging of the barge's bow. 'It'll keep our energy up and observation levels high.'

So Chase and I eat a block or two, and I must say it does seem to have hit the spot, because after we've listened to some cheerful German beer-drinking tunes, some soppy songs from *Cats*, and a few old favourite folksy foot-tappers from yesteryear, we say *au revoir* to the Eiffel Tower and *bonjour* to some brown and white cows!

'*Yes*,' says Chase with satisfaction, looking out over the dark green countryside, 'we really are *cruisin*'!'

CHAPTER FORTY

Chase and I take turns steering the *Solange*, and even Isobel gives it a go – once she's calmed down, admitting that Amy and I had no choice, really, but to set sail to escape Roland. So as the afternoon sun turns everything golden, it seems the world has slowed to the natural rhythms of the French countryside where cows and sheep graze and clouds pass steadily overhead.

'Where, exactly, George,' says Isobel, 'are we heading? Because this river meets the English Channel and the *Solange* isn't designed for open seas. In the old days, she used to carry stuff like wheat and apples and timber, but only along rivers and canals.'

Isobel is right. The closer we get to Le Havre, which as everyone knows, is one of the busiest sea ports in Europe, the more dangerous it will be.

'Hey skipper,' says Chase, looking out. 'There's a nice quiet-looking canal to the left. Why don't we go up there?'

We check out the tree-lined canal that is a lot smaller than the Seine. Its water is black and only flows gently. A couple of horses stand at the edge, one drinking, one watching us.

'Why not?' I say, and slow-turn the *Solange* into this lovely but lonely-looking waterway. 'It'll confuse Roland, which is a grand idea.'

Isobel studies the small stone farmhouses that stand in green fields lined with tall, straight poplar trees.

'It's like a poem coming to life,' she says dreamily. 'I'm going up on deck. I want to smell the grass and look at those lovely cows!'

She leaves the wheelhouse and Amy goes with her. Chase and I take turns at the wheel, both of us keeping a lookout for anything, including Roland, that might endanger us or the barge.

'At some point, we have to moor,' I say. 'Because it'll be dark soon.'

Chase nods. 'We could always ask that old guy. See him on the bike path there?'

An old fellow on an old black bike is pedalling merrily along beside the canal. He waves and calls out.

'*Bonjour, la Solange! Bonjour, la Solange!*'

'He seems pretty friendly,' I say, and seeing an ancient wooden dock ahead, I make a decision.

'Let's take her in there, Chase. You steer, slow her down, and I'll go out and tie her up. All going well.'

I head onto the deck and stand by the bow rope in the cold dusk.

'I'll do the rope at the back,' Isobel calls out. 'That old gentleman says he'll tie it up if I can hand it across.'

Like a champion crew, we bring the *Solange* slowly into the dock, and in a minute, we have her tied at the bow, mid-ships, and stern, the engine silent, the quiet of the evening settling around us. It is, as Isobel says, like entering a dream of days-gone-by, when barges used the canals and rivers like trains use tracks. The smell of woodsmoke drifts from a distant chimney, and it's as if we have arrived in the peaceful past.

The skinny old gentleman in baggy brown trousers, standing with one hand resting on the *Solange*'s side, beams at us.

'I know *Solange*,' he says happily, his face full of cheerful wrinkles. 'Eet was my father's boat. I work on 'er very 'ard. She iz beautiful. I 'ave not seen 'er for sixty years.' Then the old fellow does a little jig on the dock, which excites Amy no end. 'God bless *la Solange*!'

As I have said before, things do just keep on getting stranger every day.

'Do you want to come on board?' Isobel asks, obviously not worried about the more senior categories of stranger-danger that we were told about in my Kids-Caring-For-But-Not-Touching-Goldfish class. 'To see her? I'm sure she's changed.'

'That would be vairy nice, *merci*,' the old boy says, and steps nimbly aboard to look around at the painted steelwork and polished timber deck. 'She iz zo beautiful now. I cannot believe she 'az come back. It iz a miracle.'

I'll say it's a miracle, especially with me, Chase, and Amy at the wheel!

'We sail 'er all over France,' the old fellow says. 'She worked and worked and worked.'

'Come inside,' Isobel says. 'Would you like a cup of tea?'

'Or coffee, of course,' I put in. 'It would only take me a minute to get the machine up and go—'

'I *don't* think so, George.' Isobel sends me a look that appears designed to knock that idea firmly on the head. '*Tea* will be fine.'

So we go into the saloon, sit down, and give Jean-Pierre Marc Alain Jean-Pierre a cup of tea.

'Ooh la la,' he says, checking out the saloon. 'You 'ave couches and pain-tings by artistes.' He points to the upside-down-possibly-sideways-maybe-even-inside-out Picasso lady. 'That one iz a liddle strange but vairy nice.' Then he cautiously pokes a cushion as if it is a wasp nest. 'Life was 'ard in ze old days. I sleep on potatoes. But good.' He takes in a long snort of air. 'Freedom, wiz room to breathe!'

Isobel listens intently. After a year in a city hospital, life on the canals and rivers, travelling slowly through the French countryside, must sound like heaven.

'I know all ze water round 'ere,' Jean-Pierre says, and slurps his tea. 'Even places where nobody evair goes anymore.'

Chase looks at me. 'That could be handy.' Then he briefly outlines our . . . *predicament* to Jean-Pierre. 'So we have to stay a step ahead of this Roland until my father sorts things out.'

Jean-Pierre nods. 'I underztand. My father, 'e alzo got 'imzelf into a money pickle once or twize. Well, a lot of money pickles, actually. So. I will keep my eyes open for zis bad-boy Roland.'

'We would appreciate that,' Isobel says. 'You're very kind.'

Jean-Pierre leans forward. 'You can rely on me. Zere are places only I know because I am vairy old and I love zis canal and all of ze French countryside.'

Outside, I see dusk is turning into darkness, darkness that will hide us from Roland – or hide Roland from us.

'Thank you for ze tea.' Jean-Pierre slowly gets up. 'Stay 'ere tonight. I come and zee you off in ze morning.' We follow the old fellow out onto the deck. 'Zis canal, it is called Canal Dix. She can take you all ze way to Italy.'

We look at each other. *Italy!* Boy, another country we could enter illegally!

'We'll work things out tomorrow,' Chase says. 'It's been very nice to meet you, Jean-Pierre.'

Jean-Pierre steps onto the dock and picks up his black bike. I am concerned that he doesn't have a helmet, because I can assure anybody interested in bicycle safety (and that should be all of us) that a beret will not protect you from much more than a low-speed collision with a low-hanging apple.

'I will 'elp.' Jean-Pierre rings his rusty bicycle bell. 'We talk in ze morning! *Bonne nuit,* my young friends. Slip well!'

We say goodbye and Jean-Pierre wobbles away up the path, into the night that is now lit by a moon that shines through the branches of an old oak tree. I look down the inky waterway and hope that Roland can't see in the dark. Of course, these days you can quite easily buy something called a torch. And if he purchased one with a xenon bulb, well!

Trouble.

'Come on, Amy,' I say. 'I'll take you onto the dock so you can visit the toilet before bed.'

We step off the *Solange* and walk along the old wooden platform. The sky is sprinkled with northern hemisphere stars that I don't recognise, which reminds me that there's a lot I *don't* know about the world. It also reminds me how far away I am from home. Then I think of my parents working hard at making the world a better place for humans and the environment, and I hope, one day, to do the same.

'Come on, Amy,' I say. 'Better get back on board.' We go back to our cabin on this magnificent ninety-year-old barge that is still going strong. And there, gratefully, we hit the hay.

Tomorrow, I think to myself just before I fall asleep, *will be another adventure. Because if we're ever to get home, something incredible will have to happen.*

CHAPTER FORTY-ONE

We get up at sunrise, hit the showers, and meet in the saloon for breakfast.

'Right, who wants a coffee?' I wander over to the machine to get things started. 'I'll just hit the old button and set my sights on ninety-two degrees Celsius.'

'Take it easy on the coffee, George,' Isobel says. 'It can be quite addictive.'

'Isobel,' I say, 'might I inform you, as we have a few minutes while the water heats up, that in worldwide clinical trials, coffee consumption at reasonable levels is considered quite beneficial.'

'Perhaps you should wait until later,' she says. 'You know you get a little over-enthusiastic if you drink it too early.'

Disappointed, I settle for hot chocolate, which is wonderful in and of itself but no substitute for the brilliant bean that stimulates the brain and opens the blood vessels like the sluice gates of the Hume

Weir on the mighty Murray River. And I can most certainly say that there are no other beans I've ever had that come close to doing that, including home-grown butter beans, or the rather cheerfully-named-but-ultimately-boring green runner bean.

So I enjoy a caffeine-free breakfast. I then do the caffeine-free dishes, and clean my caffeine-free teeth with caffeine-free toothpaste. Then we go out onto the *Solange*'s sunny deck, dew sparkling in the grass on the riverbanks, sheets of gold lying on the surface of the canal, and simply enjoy the delights of the caffeine-free morning with all of my five major senses unsensitised.

'Check it out.' Chase points down the canal path. 'It's old Jean-Pierre. And he looks to be in a bit of a hurry.'

We watch as Jean-Pierre wobbles dangerously along the dock on his bike and stops with a squeak of brakes.

'A vairy fast boat iz on ze big rivair,' he says, in between wheezy breaths. 'The people in it are asking everybody if zay 'ave seen *Solange*. I zink you better 'ead upstream. Otherwise you will be capturized and zat will be zat, I zink.'

That certainly would be that, if Roland has any say.

'Start her up, Georgie-boy.' Chase gives me the nod. 'Izzy and I'll throw off the ropes, then we'll charge full-speed ahead upstream.'

Jean-Pierre's wrinkled face wrinkles more and more until his black eyes disappear. Then they flash open, filled with a wild joy.

'I will 'elp!' He lifts off his plum-coloured beret. 'I will come on *Solange* and zhow you where you can 'ide her.' He laughs, claps, and does his little jig. 'Zo exciting! An adven-ture! Let's go!'

'Okay, Jean-Pierre,' says Chase. 'Quick. Jump on board and let's get out of here. Yo, Georgie, do your thing!'

Did Chase mean turn on the coffee machine? Or start the engine?

Well, me being Thorough George, I'll do both, so I nip back into the saloon, turn the coffee machine on as I'm passing, and then climb into the wheelhouse. I hit the green starter button, and off we go, heading for the Italian border at seven kilometres an hour, Amy barking like crazy at this absolutely insane breakneck speed.

Jean-Pierre takes over the helm. 'I know ze water, Monsieur George. I can make la *Solange* go fazter. Why don't you build yourzelf a coffee while ze going iz good?'

Yes, why don't I? So I go downstairs and get into coffee-making action like a well-caffeinated machine.

'You never know when we might get another chance, Isobel,' I say, handing her a latte with a froth daffodil tied with a froth bow. 'This is just being sensible, which is a life-skill I specialise in.'

'Oh, yes, George.' Isobel takes her coffee and gives me a look I can only describe as *cool*. 'Very sensible.'

I take that as a signal to ramp up production, although I must admit I have had a few sneaky sips – well, a few sneaky *cups* – just to see if this new packet of beans is up to my incredibly high barista standards.

'No worries at *all*.' I whip up a flat white for Chase, a long black for Jean-Pierre, a pupaccino for Amy, and an Appaloosa for me, which is my own invention of a short black triple shot with seventeen spots of cream that give a dappled effect like the horse of that name. Then I whack in a sugar, as I am that kind of a guy, and slurp it down. 'See, Isobel?'

I put down the empty cup. 'No effect. Not on young George. *No* way.'

Isobel turns off the machine. 'Go and see what Jean-Pierre's plan is. I'll pack our stuff. In case we have to leave in a hurry.'

'Right on!' I shoot up the ladder, jump into the seat next to Jean-Pierre, then pick up Amy and put her in her favourite place with paws on the dashboard and her nose against the windscreen. 'So what's the plan, JP? Because right now, it's *go* time!'

Jean-Pierre concentrates on the canal, looking over Amy's pointy black ears. Suddenly, I hear church bells chiming. Amy has hit *Rock 'n' Roll Christmas Classics*, which, although spiritually uplifting, is rather inappropriate in a tense situation occurring quite some weeks after December the twenty-fifth. I turn down the volume but leave the music on, as Amy seems to be enjoying it.

'I am 'eading for an old canal called ze Lozt River,' Jean-Pierre says. 'It iz covaired wiz treez, George. *Solange* can stay in zaire for a short while. Or a long while.'

'*Sweet!*' I say. 'I'll just go downstairs and check out the situation.' I slide down the ladder and decide that, although I don't know much about art, we absolutely must take the Picasso picture with us. Especially if it's worth upwards of thirty million buckeroos.

Chase comes into the saloon as I climb onto the couch.

'What's up, Georgie-boy? You dusting the pictures, old bean?'

'If we have to abandon ship,' I explain, 'we should take this picture. It's worth millions.'

Chase agrees. 'There's bubble wrap in the galley. Grab that.'

So off I toddle at about seventy kilometres an hour, and wrap the wonky painted lady as if she's intended as a birthday present for Christmas 2060. Then I go out on deck.

'I think I can hear a speedboat,' Chase says.

With my caffeine-enhanced hearing, I pick up the distant whine of twin outboard motors, most probably Mercury 250s.

'Unless someone's doing some water-skiing at this ungodly hour, Chase,' I say, 'that'll be our boy, Roland. I'll go tell Johnny-P.'

Chase nods. 'I'll help Isobel get our stuff. See you in a minute.'

He darts off, tapping into his phone as he goes. Then I whiz back inside and fly up the ladder.

'We've got trouble,' I tell Jean-Pierre. 'There's a speedboat coming up behind us at high speed. Which is what they do.'

Jean-Pierre nods grimly. ''E will catch us before ze Lozt River Canal. Perhaps you can jump off and jump on a train to anothair country, Gheorge. Pozzibly Ruzzia.'

Oh, I'd prefer not Russia, but then again, it might be nice to visit Siberia and see what all the fuss is about.

'Good plan, Jean-Pierre!' I slide down the ladder with Amy under one arm and rush back out on deck, where Isobel stands with our luggage.

'That boat's getting close,' she says. 'But we're ready to go. If we have anywhere *to* go.'

I tell Chase and Isobel about Jean-Pierre's idea to hide the *Solange* up the Lost River Canal.

'Okay . . .' Chase looks at his phone then at Isobel and me. 'But we won't jump off quite yet. Because Plan C is just about to come online.'

'Plan C?' I run through the alphabet forwards then backwards in one-point-eight seconds. 'Did I miss Plan B, Chase? Perhaps over the vibrations of the coffee grinder? Boy, I'll have to get that thing looked at, then, because I prefer a finer blend than—'

'Plan *Clementine.*' Chase shuts his phone. 'But her phone's dropped out. So we'll just have to wait to see what happens.'

I hear the high-pitched roar of powerful twin outboard motors, and around the bend zooms a black inflatable boat. It is captained by Roland and crewed by Olga and Katerina, all three in black wetsuits.

'You are up zis French crick wiz no peddle, 'orrible Gheorge!' Roland shouts through a megaphone. 'You are cornaired like a feelthy ret or an untidy mouze and muzt give up! And alzough ze conzequencez will be terrible, zat is ze funniezt bit for me.'

'Listen!' Isobel stands still. 'Something big is coming downstream!'

I certainly can hear something powerful coming fast. It's the *chop-chop-chop* of a chopper!

'It's *Clemmy!*' Chase goes down on one knee, holding his phone, and pumps a fist. 'And here she comes!'

Just metres above the water, a big dark blue helicopter comes screaming down Canal Dix, straight at the barge. Behind us, Roland's boat is at the *Solange*'s stern – that is, until Jean-Pierre puts the wheel hard-over and pushes the black boat right up onto the bank and three wet-suited maniacs are tossed out into the reeds! Jolly good show!

The helicopter hovers right over us and the noise is incredible, the downdraft pushing us onto the deck as it starts to descend. Chase shouts:

'GET OUT OF THE WAY! CLEMMY'S BRINGING IT IN!'

We scramble back to the wheelhouse as the Jet Ranger settles like an enormous bird of prey, the *Solange* now wedged across the canal. The side door of the helicopter slides open and a helmeted crewman holds out a gloved hand to help Isobel aboard as we throw in our bags.

Chase shouts in my ear. 'Go, Georgie! Take the painting! Go!'

Well, I would, but Amy has been blown away up the *Solange*'s deck.

'No, you go!' I shout back. 'Take the picture!' I hand over the Wonky Lady. 'Give me ten seconds!'

Chase scrambles into the chopper and I crawl after Amy, suddenly seeing Jean-Pierre crawling the other way! He scoops Amy up and holds her out.

'Fly away, liddle Gheorgie and tiny Amee! I will 'ide ze *Solange*. Come back one day and meet me at L'Hotel Fat Rabbit! Jean-Pierre will live thirty more yearz because coffee beanz keep me young! *Bon voyage*, my good friend!'

'I hear you, daddio,' I shout back. 'Thanks for everything, Jean-Pierre! *Merci!*'

I turn and see Roland and the Russians climbing like black spiders up over the stern of the barge. Time for Georgie to fire his jets! Down the deck I run, Amy under one arm, only to see that the helicopter is lifting off.

'Grab on, Geepy!' Chase holds out a hand. 'We're going!'

I toss Amy to Isobel then grab Chase's arm. For one dizzying moment, I am dangling in mid-air – but not to worry, I'm coffee-cool with it, as they say! Then I'm in the chopper, Clemmy hits the power, and the *Solange* falls away as we lift like a rocket into the sky.

'Holy smoke, space cadets!' Chase throws himself back in his seat. 'That was freakin' awesome!'

'Oh, Clemmy,' Isobel says, talking to our life-saving pilot. 'You are the best girl in the world.'

Clemmy shrugs, her eyes invisible behind dark aviator sunglasses, her blonde hair hidden under a white space-age helmet.

'I'll drop you guys on the yacht,' she replies. 'I have to have this thing back in London by lunchtime.'

Isobel sits down. 'I have a feeling, Chase,' she says, 'that our lives are about to change. Again.'

CHAPTER FORTY-TWO

Fifteen minutes later, Clemmy circles a large white yacht in a dark green sea. Then in we go, dropping towards a painted H in the middle of the helipad.

'No more Roland,' I say. 'Unless he intends to swim the English Channel.'

Amy barks as we descend smoothly. Looking down, I see a small crowd of people waiting.

'Someone,' says Isobel, 'has a fair bit of explaining to do. And it's not us.'

Oh, good, I think, because although I'm a Sudoku specialist and a serial winner of the annual Tapley Chess Essay, Poem, Riddle, Limerick, and Bush Ballad Competition, I'd need weeks to work out whether what we've done is good, bad, legal, or illegal.

'All clear, guys,' Clemmy says as the helicopter settles. 'Please check your seat pockets in front and take any personal belongings. Then heads down and out you get. See you soon. Stay safe.'

We thank her, hop out, and turn to watch as the Jet Ranger lifts off and heads for London. Then, as Chase and Isobel hug their parents, I step back, because when the questions start, I do not want to be the one who has to come up with the answers.

'You're a *Tapley* boy, George?' Mr Landon-Bond wears a safari hunter's shirt with sewn-in loops for bullets, or perhaps carrots, for the more approachable species of wildlife. 'On the Landon-Bond Scholarship? You've got a big future, that's for *sure*.'

I'm not so sure. In fact, all I want from the future is to get back to school, or home, and think things through. Oh, and sort out a coffee machine and a decent grinder.

'We're so grateful you helped the children, George.' Mrs Landon-Bond wears a black-and-white dress and a flat white hat with a long black ribbon. 'Now we're just one happy family! Izzy looks *so* well.'

I nod and smile, because I can't see the point of doing anything else.

'She's very well now,' I say. 'She's probably the *wellest* person I know. And she's brilliant, brave, gifted, talented, and wonderful.'

Isobel pats my shoulder and smiles her lovely Isobel smile.

'You're the best, George. Perhaps you'd like a coffee?'

Perhaps I most certainly, definitely, positively would!

Chase and I share a cabin that is quite luxurious. It has two huge beds and a white marble bathroom complete with twin baths, ten gold taps, and twelve blue towels the size of tents.

'I'd better make the most of this.' Chase lies on a bed against eight pillows, his hands behind his head. 'Because my dad has sold every house we have, and just about everything we own to keep those guys off our backs. And keep himself out of every international court in the world.'

I sit on my bed, enjoying the sensation of the waves but not enjoying hearing Chase outline his family's misfortunes. He doesn't mention the words *bankruptcy* or *criminal charges*, but I get the feeling that they may well be on or under the tip of his tongue.

'What about the Wonky Lady picture, Chase?' It sits in the corner of our cabin, wrapped up, safe and sound. 'That thing's worth millions.'

Chase crosses his feet. 'She's already sold, Georgie-boy. On Art-Bay. Proceeds are with Miss J in Tokyo, who'll use it for a fighting fund to keep us out of jail.'

'Oh,' I say. 'Boy, there sure must be a lot of money going around this world that normal people don't know about. It's rather confusing.'

'Too true, Geepy. Too true.' Chase pounds a pillow for extra comfort. 'The Landon-Bonds are a bunch of falling stars, burnt-out and broke, crashing back to earth.' He looks at me. 'Remember those kids we sponsored in Africa, Geeps? All two thousand of them or whatever?'

I experience a sad and serious sinking feeling. Without the money Chase promised, I wonder how their lives might be? I mean, drinking fresh water and going to school should be the right of every kid in the world, and that's one of my ambitions – to see that happens.

'I remember, Chase.' I think of those children looking hopefully into the camera, smiling, thinking we were able to help. 'The ones we got the trophy for, for being the world's best sponsors.'

'Yep, them,' Chase says. 'Well, buddy-boy, I pre-paid a million bucks into the account. So they'll be fine until they leave school. And the orang-utans and Terry the tiger have got a hundred thousand each. Three done deals. Locked in, locked down, locked tight. *Boom!*'

I look at Chase, seeing a wonderful, smart, daring, and generous kid from a strange world of double-deals, mega deals, bad deals, bad deeds, and, in this case, a good deed multiplied by millions.

'You're a great guy, Chase,' I say. 'I'm going to nominate you for school captain.'

Chase throws me a handmade chocolate the size of a tennis ball. An eight-kilogram box of them was delivered to us from Eduardo, the Brazilian gazillionaire who owns the yacht we're on.

'Not sure which school that might be, George.' Chase peels off the gold foil that is actually made from real gold. 'I won't be going back to Tapley. We're broke, bro.'

'You can have my scholarship money,' I say promptly. 'My local school's good. I can live at home and walk there, watched all the way by my mother through her telescope, or night-vision goggles, if it's a particularly overcast day. Consider it done.'

Chase sits up. 'I appreciate it, Geeps. But we might both be going to new schools, because the

Landon-Bond Scholarship has run out of puff. It won't even buy you lunch.'

No more Tapley for either of us! Then it strikes me that I don't really care — or not as much as I thought I would. Of course, I'll miss the lads at the Chargers, my little room that has a window to the stars, and having the private use of three libraries, four science labs, and a state-of-the-art language centre that the Tapley boys and teachers never go near.

'Oh, well,' I say. 'I wasn't ever going to be a very good rower or clay pigeon shooter, was I?'

'Yeah, well, *whatever* to all that stuff.' Chase grins. 'You're still the best kid, Georgie. And whatever does happen, and wherever we do go, we'll always be mates, won't we?'

'That,' I say, 'would be very nice.'

'Right on, sport.' Chase nods. 'Because the future's a great place and we should look forward to it. We'll make things happen. All we've got to do is use our imagination and hang in there.'

I've never understood what the expression 'Hang in there' actually refers to. I'd suggest perhaps it would have something to do with conquering the monkey bars, because if you don't *hang in there*, or *hang on there*, you might find yourself in a tiny room with a large school nurse with very cold hands, which I can personally report is something to be avoided.

'Yes,' I say, and daringly add, 'we will hang up, I mean, *in*, there.'

CHAPTER FORTY-THREE

Eduardo, Mr Landon-Bond's friend, has offered his private jet to fly us home to Australia from London. I am not, of course, used to anything like this; at our house, my dad's friend, Lambert, might lend us a power drill, if my dad knew how to use one, but not a Lear jet. No point complaining, though. We simply waltz through British customs, me carrying Amy, and get on board. And in seven minutes, we are out of English airspace, hitting a thousand kilometres an hour.

'Here we go, George.' Chase looks out his window as we burst through clouds and into bright sunlight. 'Back to the *really* real world. I'm looking forward to it. It'll be a challenge. Rich kid no more.'

'It won't be a challenge for you, Chase,' I suggest. 'You can do anything. You're smart, funny, and great at sport. You'll always do well and have fun.'

Chase pats Amy. 'We'll see. But I'm pretty sure that no miracles, financial or educational, will be happening any time soon. From here on in, the Landon-Bonds are on their own.'

Isobel leans forward. 'Have you heard any more news on your Super Algae, George?'

Funnily enough, I have. In an Australian paper the onboard jet butler provided, there is an article about an outbreak of algae flowing out of a *very* familiar-looking inner-Melbourne backyard. Evidently two fire engines got bogged in it, and a team of scientists have been called in to see exactly what sort of algae it might be.

'It seems to be going quite well,' I say. 'As far as exceeding its growth targets go.'

'You might save the world, George.' Isobel rubs Amy's small black ears. 'Like you saved Amy. And me.'

'And me, at times,' adds Chase.

'We all saved each other,' I say emphatically. 'With the help of many other great people. And that's the truth.' I glance towards the rear of the plane where the kitchen is. 'Do you think they have coffee? Because when I get home, it'll be all half-strength decaffeinated soy lattes stirred with bamboo slivers and served in cold cups once a week. And Barista George *cannot* go there.'

'Of course they have coffee.' Chase snaps his fingers. 'Eduardo's Brazilian, Georgie-boy. He owns the biggest coffee plantation in the world.'

Oh, that's handy!

CHAPTER FORTY-FOUR

We arrive in Melbourne on a clear day, the city looking wonderful as a black limousine takes us in towards Chase's mansion in Toorak.

'If your parents are away, George,' Isobel says. 'Stay with us. We don't have to leave our house for two weeks.'

'Thank you, Isobel.' My parents are still in Switzerland. 'I'll only stay for a night or two,' I add. 'Then I'll go to my place.'

Chase gives me a companionable whack. 'Tomorrow, old boy,' he informs me, 'we'll go down to Tapley on the train to get our stuff. No more limos for the Landon-Bonds. It's public transport all the way, every day.'

'Oh, *please*, Chase,' says Chase's dad, who wears a slick grey suit and two large gold watches. 'It's only temporary. If we can go from riches to rags overnight, then I can't see a problem heading back the other way in the same time-frame.'

'From now on, Dad,' Isobel puts in, 'Chase and I are going to be involved in everything this family does. We're old enough and smart enough to see some of the things we should do and not do in the future.'

Mrs Landon-Bond puts a slender hand loaded with diamonds and rubies on Isobel's slender hand that has no jewellery at all.

'You need to rest, Isobel, rather than think about things that don't interest you.'

Isobel retracts her hand. 'Oh, but they do interest me. And I should have been a lot more interested a lot earlier on, and we wouldn't be in the situation we are now. I'm sick of resting. I'm ready to get to work, school, and study.'

Silence settles like mist until Chase claps.

'*Exactly*, Isobel,' he says. 'From now on the Landon-Bonds are going to be thoughtful, responsible, helpful and . . . er . . . careful. Or a little more careful than we have been. We will earn our money honestly. Then no one can take it off us.'

'Bravo, Chase.' Mr Landon-Bond nods as we are taken up the driveway of their huge house, which isn't theirs any more. 'Meanwhile, anyone for tennis? I believe we have the coaching team for another week.'

CHAPTER FORTY-FIVE

Chase and I catch a train and bus to Tapley Grammar. Walking towards school, I see the honey-coloured stone buildings rising from the ovals and the horses of the Tapley equestrian and polo teams gazing over the white wooden fences.

'I'll miss this place,' Chase says. 'I liked it here.'

'So did I.' I feel like a stranger now. This school isn't our school anymore. 'But that's how the cookie crumbles.'

Chase laughs. 'It is, Parkie. Anyway, let's go see the headmaster. I'm sure he'll be impressed with your current hairstyle.'

My Mohawk is really no longer a true Mohawk. It looks like a line of pale shrubbery growing over a partially grassed hill in the middle of summer.

'I was thinking,' I say, 'of going into town to see Maddylynne at Klassicke Kutz. To say goodbye and get a more George-appropriate hairstyle.'

'I'll come with you.' Chase and I head on up the

stairs to the Tapley Administration Centre, Stock Market, and Satellite Monitoring Facility. 'We'll check out, get our stuff, then we'll walk into town. And *then* we'll make a break for the big city.'

I go up to my room, thinking about the scholarship that the headmaster offered me, but I won't accept it. What fun would this place be without Chase? So even as I am on my way into my room, I'm on my way out. Nothing in the little wooden space has changed, I see, except perhaps me.

'Ha,' I murmur. 'Well, well, well.'

I pack my books and things, moving around the dusty room that has been like a close and protective friend. And when I'm done, I look down on the beautiful Sir Roger Blackheart Buccaneer Oval and although I am sad, maybe I'm a little relieved, too. Yes, I suppose I do love this place but that doesn't mean I won't love other places. Picking up my bag, I see on the floor the 1930 penny I found at the old coffee house all those weeks ago.

'Hmmm,' I say, looking at it. 'So what to do with you, my valuable little round friend?'

I put the penny in my safest pocket then leave,

quietly closing the door. At the top of the stairs, I consider sliding down the banister – which would be utter madness, as that has resulted in the deaths of fifteen Tapley boys, some of whom supposedly still wander the corridors at night, moaning about bank accounts they can no longer access. So slowly and sensibly, I head down the stairs to meet Chase.

We walk through the Tapley grounds then along the beach into town. I look around for that girl Charlotte, but she's nowhere to be seen. So all I can do is hope she writes her book and has a lovely life.

'No sign of Charlotte,' I say as we pass the empty jetty.

'Not this time,' Chase replies. 'Pity. She's a great kid. And she likes you.'

We make it into town, me realising with sadness that I'm about to go in to Klassicke Kutz to see Maddylynne for the last time.

'Meet you at the jetty, Chase,' I suggest. 'Say, in an hour?'

'Got it, dude.' Chase gives me the thumbs-up. 'Make sure Maddylynne gives you something truly radical, bro.'

'Yes,' I call back. 'I won't!'

And I don't.

I simply ask Maddylynne to basically cut all my hair to the one short length, which she does. Then I give her flowers, because she's always been very nice to me, and I get out of there quickly, before I cry, because it seems a lot of wonderful things are coming to an end.

'See you, George!' She calls out from the front step, wearing her yellow apron, holding her clippers. 'You're a good person!'

'So are you, Maddylynne,' I call back. 'Thank you for everything!'

I walk along the beach, the Tapley buildings looking like something from a dream that I am walking towards but also away from, which is an appealing concept, if not a little paradoxical, but then that's life.

'Hi, George!'

I look towards the sand dunes and I see a girl walk out onto the beach. It's Charlotte and she has on jeans, a loose white shirt, and a bag slung over her shoulder.

'Charlotte!' I say, and feel something bump in my chest as we meet by the water. 'How are you?'

She smiles. 'I'm good, George. I saw you and Chase walk past so I rushed down to see how you are. So where have you been?'

'Where have I been?' I make a circle in the air with an index finger. 'I've been to quite a few places. One day I'll tell you, Charlotte. One day I will. How's your book going?'

She reaches into her shoulder bag and takes out five writing pads held together with rubber bands.

'I've written two hundred and seventy-seven pages.' She shows me. 'All by hand. But I need a computer to write it out properly. And we can't afford one. So I'm not sure what to do.'

'Well, I'm sure,' I say, as I reach into my safest pocket and take out my King George 1930 penny, 'that if you take this coin to a coin expert, Charlotte, he will give you a lot of money. And then you can buy a computer.'

Charlotte shakes her head, her coppery hair shimmering. 'I couldn't take it, George. It's yours.'

'It's not mine, not really,' I reply. 'It was just lying on a floor in an old building waiting for someone to come along. Take it, Charlotte.'

And that's what happens. Well, actually there's a bit more to it than that – she takes the coin, we give each other our home telephone numbers and we smile at each other.

Yes, that's what happens.

And I'm quite pleased that it does!

Chase and I leave Tapley for the last time, catch the bus under the old oak tree, and arrive at the railway station. There we sit in the waiting room and not much seems to be happening, but, as my dad says, nothing is never happening, meaning something is happening all the time. And my dad is right, because the headline on the front page of the *Melbourne Financial Times* states:

Amazing Algae Will Save the World!

The picture below shows a river of green algae flowing out the front gate of Number Twelve Poorly Street, which is *my* house, and continues on down the road out of sight!

'Oh my goodness, Chase,' I say. 'That's my place and that's my algae! Wow. It seems to have had something of a growth spurt while we've been away.'

'And not only that, Georgie,' says Chase, turning his phone around. 'Look.' He shows me a picture of a person in a laboratory holding a test tube that looks like an algae fountain! 'Read this, dude.'

'I can't, Chase,' I say. 'I don't have my glasses.'

'Oh, okay.' Chase takes a deep breath. 'It says: "Parker Algae 2000 creates mega-million bio-fuel bonanza for creator".' He looks at me. 'You know what that means, don't you?'

'No,' I answer. 'Not really.'

'It means,' Chase jumps up, 'you're a bio-fuel billionaire, George! You're possibly the *richest* kid in the world! What are you gonna *do* with *all* that money?'

I have to think about that as I've never, ever, been rich before. Then the ideas start to flow.

'I'm going to *save* the Tasmanian devil,' I say. 'I'm going to *send* Isobel to art school. I'm going to *buy* a coffee machine. I'm going to give my parents their own lab! I'm going to buy a thousand copies of Charlotte's book! And you and I, Chase, will *find* the *Solange*, visit the kids in Africa, the tiger in India, and the orang-utans in Borneo! And,' I smile at my best friend 'that's just the beginning, Chase. That is *just* the beginning!'

ABOUT THE
AUTHOR

David Metzenthen lives in Melbourne with his family and pets. He loves writing for young readers and has written more than forty books, some very short, some rather long. He has won five Premier's Literary Awards, a Prime Minister's Award, and was awarded a Children's Book Council of Australia Book of the Year Award. He hopes you enjoy George Parker's story as much as he enjoyed creating the incredible young George!